The Living, The Dead, and The Unwed

The Living, The Dead, and The Unwed

TYRANNY HOVEY

For my family who has to listen to all my crazy-I love you all and most days wouldn't trade you.

Bullock- You will always be first. Everyone should have a cheerleader like you.....no I don't need pics of you in the uniform.

1

Chapter 1

I've seen the living; I've seen the dead. I've seen angels and I've seen demons. No matter how many malevolent or benevolent beings I interacted with, none could terrify me as much as the spirit that walked through the laundry room door into the kitchen where I was cooking dinner. Mentally bracing myself, I stirred in chili powder to the ground beef on the stove before I acknowledged the woman that was now looking over my shoulder.

"That's too much seasoning. It's going to be too spicy." Somehow, I kept the sigh to myself as I turned to face the food police. She was fairly tall, white hair wrapped around her head in an intricate braid, with her superior complex obvious in her blue eyes. "You need to call your mother." It was an order, not a request. I raised an eyebrow, inviting her to explain. "She won't listen to reason."

"Are you two still feuding?" Grandma Eleanor had been dead for three years now. She had been fighting with my mother for the last two and a half years.1 I'd inherited the "gift" from my mother who had gotten it from my grandmother and so on and so forth. They didn't need me to pass messages back and forth. Nope, she wanted me to take her side against my mother. She seemed to have forgotten that I had refused to get involved.

"She has no right to do what she's doing! She won't listen to me, but she'll listen to you. Maybe you should go over there and tell her." She made a shooing motion with her hands. "Go on now, that chili isn't going to be fit to eat anyways. Why won't you just go to those cooking classes I suggested?"

Careful not to touch the lenses on my glasses, I pinched my nose. I heard the garage door rattle up followed by the roar of a v-8 engine. Moments later, my husband stepped into the dining room from the garage with a barely concealed smirk. The look I sent him was a little less warm than normal. His dark blonde covered head with the features on the delicate side was welcome, his green eyes with that knowing glint in them was not. He couldn't see the dead or non-human entities like I could, his gifts laid in energies. While he couldn't see grandma, he could feel her and read my irritation. He swung his gaze to where my grandmother stood before addressing the empty space in front of the dishwasher.

"Eleanor, always good to see you." His eyes swung back to me while he deposited his laptop bag on the dining room table. She glared at my husband, hard to say if it was because she had no sense of humor or because she never approved of my marrying a psychic instead of a medium. She always thought I'd married beneath my station, that I should have married a medium like she had.

"I'll be downstairs." He headed down the hall to the pit of denial AKA the lower floor of our split-level house he had converted to his man cave after our eight-year-old daughter proclaimed Joe Jonas the hottest man on earth. He'd added a pool table and jukebox when she had hit puberty.

"Coward!" I yelled at his rapidly retreating back. He flashed me a flirty smile then disappeared behind the basement door. A throat being cleared returned my attention to my ghostly visitor. "If you have something to say to mom, pop over there and talk to her yourself."

"Holly Lee Bush! You know how unreasonable your mother can be when it comes to me. She will listen to you." I threw her an irritated look.

"Leefe. Holly Lee Bush Leefe. If you must use my full name, don't forget the one I actually go by." Leefe wasn't much of an upgrade from Bush, but it did reduce the number of jokes. The double entendres had gotten old before high school. Growing up in Texas with the last name of Bush hadn't been easy either. I sniffed the air. "No no no!" Quickly I spun around to the stove. I'd been so distracted I'd forgotten to turn down the heat on the chili. The bottom of the pan felt like a bumpy back road when I tried to stir the bubbling mess. Well dinner was ruined. Guess we would be having sandwiches.

"They have cooking classes at the Y." Grandma Eleanor dissipated after her parting shot. With a growling sound, I dumped the chili down the drain then started cleaning up the mess.

Meanwhile at a house in Grapevine

Libby Walker sat on her plush vanity bench staring into the three mirrors on the vanity, tweezers in hand looking for any unwanted facial hair. Not seeing any hair that needed plucked, she began checking her roots to see if her natural brown was showing. Currently she had colored it gray. The color was popular among the young women. She was certain that she looked young enough to wear it. Content that all hairs were as they should be, she loaded her favorite TikTok makeup channel to practice the new eye liner styles.

Michael Cook felt a shiver as he entered the house. The AC felt chilly after spending the last few hours cleaning the flowerbeds in the courtyard. Carefully he slipped off his work boots, placing them upside down on the shoe hooks by the garage door. Once his house shoes were on his feet, he padded across the laminate floor to the bathroom. As he washed his hands, splashing the water on his face to cool down, he thought he heard a woman's voice in the hall. "Toots?"

Opening the door revealed an empty hall. Cocking his head, he thought he could still hear a female's voice. Maybe multiple women talking. He walked as silently as he could on floors that echoed every step. The popping of his knee brought him to a halt. The voices stilled as well. Mentally he chastised his old knee. They had been hearing voices for months. This could have been his chance to finally figure out the source of them. Even though she had been gone for years now, he worried that his beloved Norma Rae was jealous of his relationship with Libby.

He turned the corner into the kitchen Libby had recently remodeled. The light reflecting off the shiny new appliances sent a pang through his heart for the avocado green gas stove he had tinkered with for years to keep it running. Noting that the kitchen was empty, Michael turned the light back off. As he walked through the living room he glanced at the back door. Reflected in the glass of the door was a woman in an aqua robe. She was walking beside him. With a startled oomph, he whirled his head to the left. No one was there. Footsteps ran across the laminate floors towards the master bedroom. A terrified shriek came from the same direction.

"Libby!" Michael called as he rushed into the room where he found his spooked fiancé.

"There's a face!" Libby screamed pointing at the mirrors of her vanity. Michael looked but was unable to see anyone. "There was a face in the mirror!"

"I believe you." Michael pulled her into his arms for a reassuring hug. She burrowed her head into his chest. This convinced Michael that there was no way this was Norma. His late wife was not the type to scare or upset people. An angry shriek had him releasing Libby.

"Look at my eyes!" She was turning her head in every direction in the mirrors. It took everything he had not to laugh. During the episode Libby had drawn her eye liner up the side of her face. Angrily Libby jerked make up remover cloths out of a pack and began to wipe her face. "I'm taking a bath."

Libby filled the giant white hammock tub she had recently installed. While the tub was filling, she went to the kitchen to get a bottle of wine. Her bare feet barely made a noise as she walked across the laminate. Yet, there was an echo of high heels for every step she took. Completely creeped out, she ran into the kitchen. Once she was on the tile, the echo stopped.

"The ghost hunters will be here tomorrow. They are bringing a psychic. They should be able to find the underlying cause of this." Michael informed her. He was sitting at the table with his email open on his laptop.

She nodded as she left the room carrying a bottle of white and a glass.

I was standing at the sink scrubbing the pan, grumbling under my breath, when the ding dong of the doorbell intruded. Great, another uninvited guest. I grabbed a towel to dry my hands off as I walked across the formal living room to the front door. The peep hole revealed a young Asian standing on my doorstep holding a paper bag. With a confused smile, I opened the door.

"Can I help you?" Pulling the door shut behind me to keep the animals in, I stepped out onto the porch. The kid had probably gotten the wrong house.

"I have your Sesame Chicken, Teriyaki Chicken, and Kung Pao Chicken with three egg drop soups, six egg rolls, and crab rangoons." He held the bag out to me. Out of reflex, I took the bag containing our usual order. "Have a nice evening."

I stood there in confusion holding the bag of food while he turned and jumped on his moped in the driveway. My husband reached around me to grab the food. I followed him back into the house. "Did you order that?"

"Duh. Every time Eleanor shows up, dinner gets ruined, and we end up eating baloney sandwiches. I think our daughter deserves better than that." The overly earnest look he was wearing meant he was lying. HE didn't want a sandwich. I answered his earnest look with my don't bother trying to lie to your wife look. He smirked at me. "And don't think we haven't noticed you switched us to turkey baloney, woman. We do not approve!" He swatted my ass.

He darted for the kitchen with me hot on his heels. I launched myself on to his back and playfully bit his neck. "EWWWW! Not in the kitchen. We eat in here!" Our teenage daughter had torn herself away from her room to grace us with her presence. She barely looked up from her phone to chastise us for our PDA. My husband set the bag of food on the counter.

"Wanna climb on my front so we can really gross her out?" Our daughter flipped her dark blonde hair out of her face so we could clearly see the horror on both her face and in her green eyes. Despite her horror, she somehow kept typing.

"Jesse Leefe!" It wasn't much of an admonishment since I was giggling. Grossing out our daughter was one of our favorite activities. I let go of his neck and slid to the ground. "Savannah, get some plates and set the table. Jess, get your stuff off the table. I'll grab some drinks."

The three of us settled around the table to enjoy the evening meal. We spent a few minutes passing around containers and sauces. "So how was everyone's day?"

My question received a shrug from the teenager. Not surprising. I looked at Jess to see if he had anything to add to the conversation. "Want to hear about the new scandal in the department?"

"Uh yeah." Jesse worked for a company that researched all things occult. Unsurprisingly it was mostly young adults, conspiracy theorists, and odd balls that worked there. Plus a few like Jesse that had gifts. This meant there was tons of interesting gossip. He launched into a story of how the new receptionist had started sleeping with the manager of the cryptozoology department. Only he had failed to mention he was also sleeping with the office manager. Today the two women had discovered they were part of a triangle. Instead of going after the cheating SOB, who incidentally was married, they ended up attacking each other. First, they exchanged insults and then the office manager tried to staple the receptionist to a wall. The receptionist retaliated by three hole punching the office manager's silk blouse. It took three people to pull them apart in the end. One for each of the women and another to pull the staples that were holding their clothes together. Savannah and I were in danger of spewing our drinks out of our noses when he finished.

"Do we have plans for tomorrow night?" Jess asked when we were all done giggling.

"Not that I can think of. Why?"

"There's a house over in Grapevine that needs your help." By day I was a data analysis. By night I was a ghost hunter. I didn't investigate every supposedly haunted house. Just the ones the ghost team at Jesse's firm determined were legitimate hauntings and that my gifts would be helpful. Often times I was called in to deal with the unruly specters that were causing problems for the living. I pulled out my phone to enter the time and address into my calendar.

"Can I go?" Savannah was looking at me hopefully. She had been asking to join us on our investigations since she was old enough to understand what we did. Jesse and I exchanged looks.

"Let me check it out first." I held up a hand to delay her protest. "You know we don't want you going to haunted places that we don't know what's in there."

"But mom! Come on! What's the chances there's a demon or something dangerous in there?" She had learned how to bat those gorgeous green eyes for sure. Undoubtedly, they got her anything she wanted from the boys at school. I was immune to them since they were a mirror image of her father's. After almost twenty years together, they had lost their potency.

"Everyone loves a movie about demons. They like the scare when it attacks. It's a whole different story when you are the one being dragged down the hallway." Jesse and I both grimaced. We'd run into our fair share of nasty entities in our lives. I tried to stay away from the demonic. The last one spun me around the ceiling like a merry-go-round. I still couldn't sleep with the fan running without getting nauseous. "If it turns out to be a run of the mill ghost that just needs to talk, maybe you can go on one of the visits."

Our daughter's gifts were still developing so we weren't sure exactly what she was going to be able to do. So far, she showed signs of a blending of mine and Jesse's. She could hear the dead but barely see them. She also could make out energies faintly. Jesse could read auras at a glance; Savannah could only pick out the strongest colors in a dim halo around a person. She did seem to have his gift for being able to see residual energy on an object.

"Fine." She drug out the word so we would know she was displeased.

Once dinner was over and the kitchen cleaned, we adjourned to the living room to watch TV. Jesse and I were comfortably curled up together watching the giant screen he had recently installed on the wall. Savannah mostly played on her phone. It dinged about every thirty seconds. I had serious thoughts of flinging it out a window one day.

"Meow. Meow. Meow." Our tortoise shell cat, Galapagos came running out of the master bedroom, a sock hanging from her mouth. She darted across the living room, stopping under the dining room table. Once there, she dropped the sock, then jumped up in one of the chairs to lick herself.

"Did you leave the laundry out again?" I didn't care for the accusatory tone in my loving spouse's tone.

"Nope. I shoved the hamper back in the closet like a normal person." We'd added Galapagos to our menagerie a few months ago. She'd showed up as a stray and demanded entry. Like the soft-hearted fools we were, we took her in. Her mannerisms suggested she had been a housecat at some point, so it worked out fairly well. Until she started dragging laundry around. Socks were her favorite. I could no longer leave my dirty clothes in a pile. My clean freak of a husband was thrilled.

"The hamper had clean clothes in it. Why didn't you put them up?" It always amused me how put out he could sound with me while twirling a strand of my hair around his finger.

"I did. I put the hamper in the closet." He rolled his eyes at me.

"Then how did she get a sock?" Normally I liked it when he whispered things in my ear, but this was not sweet nothings. I also didn't trust the fingers that were now resting on my ribs in a prime position to tickle me. In a pre-emptive move, I rolled out of his grip onto the floor. He looked over the edge of the couch at me. "That's not the actions of an innocent person."

I stuck my tongue out at him as I scrambled to my feet. He dove for me. I took off running for the bedroom. Savannah made her grossed out sounds. She and Jesse followed me into our room. I flung my arms up in victory. "See. No laundry."

"Mom, look." Savannah pointed at my dresser that, yet another giant TV sat on. There was a sock hanging out of the middle drawer.

"Oh, dear lord. She's figured out how to open and close drawers." I looked at my family in disbelief. "How does she know which drawer my socks are in?"

"I told you, there's too much intelligence in her eyes." Our daughter was convinced Galapagos was actually a human turned into a cat. We'd never found any verifiable proof that such a thing could be done. But we did have to agree that at times, she did seem to understand us.

"I looked it up. Cats use socks as prey substitutes. That's all it is. Nothing to be alarmed by." Jesse opened the drawer to tuck my sock back inside while he tried to alleviate our daughter's concern. "It's after ten, time for bed." Savannah ran from the room as he stripped off his shirt to reveal his slightly out of shape dad bod.

2

Chapter 2

The alarm went off way too early the next morning. Blurry eyed I stumbled out of bed to start my day. From the kitchen I could smell coffee and sausage. My darling spouse was already up, making breakfast and watching Scooby Doo if I wasn't mistaken.

"Overachiever." I muttered towards the kitchen as I climbed in the white wood tiled shower, water turned to just below boiling. Why had I married a morning person?

Since I'd recently chopped off my currently golden blonde hair, it only took fifteen minutes to shower and do my hair. I'd been trying to get the collar of my blouse to lie on the lapel of my jacket like it was supposed to when Jesse texted me that breakfast was ready. It would appear that I was running late like usual. I scooped up my jewelry to dash to the kitchen. Hopefully, I would have time to put it on before we left. During the short walk across the living room, I managed to hop into the hot pink heels that matched the blouse under my black jacket.

Savannah was already at the table picking at a breakfast burrito. Knowing my tendencies to be late, Jesse had wrapped my burrito in foil so it would still be warm when I got to the office in an hour or so depending on the traffic on 360. He paused his way back to our room to finish getting ready to dramatically grab me, recline me backwards, and plant one on me. We laughed as Savannah ewwwed from the kitchen.

"Mom, we need to leave in three minutes! Stop making out with dad. You're old."

"Never too old to make out. Have you seen my walker?" All I got was an eye roll. "Am I too old to drive? That would suck for you seeing as how you won't take the bus."

"If you'd just let me ride with Eddy, you wouldn't have to drop me off!" Savannah was gearing up for what was becoming a regular morning whine fest. "Then you wouldn't have to leave so early."

"Which one is Eddy again?" Names weren't really my thing. Besides, I was a little distracted trying to fasten my bracelet with my teeth while getting my lunch out of the fridge.

She sighed and rolled her eyes at me. "Jock Boy."

I sighed back. Jock Boy had game, both on and off the field. "You want me to let you ride in Jock Boy's truck? Oh, I don't think so little girl."

"Mom! I'm fifteen. Practically an adult." She sounded offended. Oh well.

I scowled at her and pointed a finger at her. "You never climb in a boy's truck. Nothing good can come from it. They just want to swap cooties."

"Eww. Mom! Gross." A gleam came into her eyes. "So, I can't ride with any boys?"

"You can ride with your daddy. No one else." My words were slightly mumbled since I had an earring back in my mouth.

"What about grandpa?" Oh, she thought she had me.

"Nope. Not since his midlife crisis and traded in his sedan for a motorcycle. He drives that thing like a madman." I inventoried my hands. Purse, phone, and lunch. Wait, something was missing.

"Has anyone seen my keys?" I was fairly certain I'd left them on the bar when I got home yesterday.

"Have you checked the key bowl by the door?" Jesse answered while walking across the living room to the dining room. He plucked my keys out of the bowl on the table by the door to the garage.

"What are they doing in there?" I tuned out his lecture about a place for everything and everything in its place. Keys in hand, I kissed my hubby goodbye then ushered our child out the door. In the garage I took a moment to stick the Jack In The Box antenna ball on Jesse's truck. I'd been waiting for him to lecture me about putting things in their proper place since I'd found it in one of our many junk drawers over the weekend. He'd hated those things when they came out years ago. But, since he said everything should be in its place, it belonged on an antenna, and it wasn't going on mine.

An hour later, the kid was dropped off; I had my morning coffee and was sitting in my office reading email trying to decide if any of them actually applied to me. When there were no new emails left, I switched over to the thrill of bouncing spreadsheets off each other.

Hours later I was dragged out of my work when my desk phone rang. The caller ID identified the caller as my mother. I took a bracing breath before I picked it up.

"Hello mother."

"Hello daughter. Savannah get to school ok?" My mother's slight southern drawl flowed through the line. Judging by the background noise, she was calling me on her way home from Zumba class. Or line dancing. I couldn't remember what she did on Thursdays. She was an active senior. We exchanged a few pleasantries before she got to the reason for her call. She was calling because her mother had stopped by this morning. Surprise surprise.

"Mom, you knew it was going to piss her off. " There was something oddly satisfying about telling my mother I told you so. More often than not, I was on the other end of it, so I relished these few times I got to be on this side.

"It's my house now! She left it to me. I can do whatever I want with it." Agitation made her voice a little higher than normal.

"I warned you before you took the putty knife to the wallpaper she would come back and that it wasn't going to be pretty. You know remodeling stirs up the dead." Finding my coffee cup empty, I pulled an energy drink out of my mini fridge. My parents had moved into the family home to take care of Grandma Eleanor after Grandpa Charles passed away. Shortly thereafter, Grandma Eleanor passed away while walking around her gardens. Six months after she had passed, mom decided it was time to update the house. My grandparents had built a grand colonial house complete with a portico in the mid-eighties. Other than routine maintenance, they hadn't updated anything. Mom chose to start the remodel by stripping the orange, avocado, and brown flower wallpaper in the kitchen. The moment she started peeling it off, I'd felt a disturbance in the force. My mother and grandmother had been at each other's throats ever since.

"Why can't she be like daddy? He pops in every once in a while. All he does is nod in approval and then pop back out. But no! She has to stand over my shoulder telling me how much it cost to have that wallpaper put in and how long it took to find that pattern. When I took down the paneling in the salon she literally shrieked in my ear."

"Tell her to leave my cabinets alone." Grandma came through the wall giving orders. I briefly wondered if she was referring to the kitchen cabinets, bathroom cabinets, or the built ins. I knew mom planned on updating all of them.

"Tell her to go back to her fiery pit and leave the living alone!" My mother hung up the phone. It was going to be one of these days.

Oh yeah. I put down the receiver before I acknowledged my ghostly visitor.

"Well, that wasn't very nice of her. She didn't get that meanness from me." She seemed out of place in the office wearing jeans and an orange plaid button up under an orange puffy vest. Her orange medium heeled boots went a little better with the business casual dress code. I'd always been grateful she hadn't died in a hospital gown with her ass showing. Doubly glad since she currently had her back to me. She had moved to the hutch where I had my Bluetooth speakers that were connected to my phone. I couldn't be sure, but I would put money on she was trying to turn off the music. She'd never cared for music. No matter the genre, it annoyed her. Giving up on turning off the music she glowered at the Funko Pop collection on display. She felt I was too old for dolls. So far, I had been unable to get her to understand collectibles came in other forms than dishware.

"Aren't you the one that taught me that this world belongs to the living and the dead are just visiting?" I took a big gulp of my drink. I was going to need as much caffeine as I could get if I was going to get drug into the middle of this. A handful of M&M's from the candy jar was needed too.

"Don't get sassy with me young lady! Your mother is destroying our family home. You should care about that. It'll be yours one day. I know how much you always loved that wallpaper." I kept my face carefully blank. If the horror I felt at the thought of that hideous paper showed on my face, I'd get a guilt trip that I did not have time to go on. "Just go to her and tell her how you want her to keep the house in its original condition."

"I'm not getting in the middle of this." I gave her a stern look. "I need to get back to work so, why don't you go talk to your daughter."

"Instead of working in a man's world, you should be at home taking care of your family. That daughter of yours wears too provocative of clothing. You should be there to teach her how to behave like a lady." A delighted look flashed across her face. "You could go to cooking classes together."

I pointed at the wall she had come through. "Get out. " She started making her hurt/shocked sounds. I knew she wasn't offended, but I didn't have time to smooth her ruffled feathers. "Don't make me get the salt."

"HMPH." She dissipated after giving me a look that promised I would pay for not immediately taking up for her. I tossed my empty can in the recycling bin, grabbed a new can, and then settled into the thrill of mining information from spreadsheets. What felt like moments later, but was actually hours according to the clock, my boss moseyed in my door to tell me goodnight.

"Just wanted to tell you bye before I left. Any plans for tonight?" Veronica had the appearance of a sweet little old grandmother with her white curly hair tumbling just below the shoulders and intelligent hazel eyes highlighted with her ever-present blue eyeshadow. I knew her to be five feet of pure fire and sci fi references. She was one of my favorite people around here.

"Heading over to Grapevine to investigate a house." She knew about and accepted my ability to communicate with the dead. Another reason I liked her. Sceptics could get so tedious.

"OOOOH. Exciting. Do you know what they are experiencing?" Her eyes had lit up like Christmas trees. It was only a matter of time until she asked to tag along on an investigation.

"Not a clue. I like to meet the spirits unbiased." I saw myself as a kind of therapist to the dead. Most just needed an interpreter, someone to pass messages between the living and the dead. The rest were either lost, unwilling to move on, or people who were malicious in life and continue to be so in death.

"Let me know tomorrow how it goes. Good night!" I waved goodbye as an alarm on my phone went off.

Shoot. I was late. Quickly I sent Jesse a text to let him know I wouldn't have time to stop by the house before heading to Grapevine. 114 was going to be a nightmare this time of day. Not wanting to wait for the elevator, I took the stairs as quickly as I could. The three flights of stairs left me winded by the time I got to the parking lot. Might be time to join the gym.

3

C hapter 3
        After fighting traffic for an hour and fifteen minutes, I turned into an older neighborhood five minutes from the Grapevine outlet mall, in a subdivision that had been built in the nineteen seventies. The presumably haunted house was a simple ranch style with a grey brick façade; the same grey bricks had been used to enclosure a small courtyard off the front porch. Jesse's white Ram sat in the driveway. Beside it was the SUV bearing his firm's name, indicating the rest of the team was already there.

I parked my purple Jeep Sahara on the street in front of the grey brick mailbox. Since I didn't want my heels sinking into the bright green grass, I walked up the driveway to the walkway that was also made out of grey brick. Whoever had built this place hadn't had much imagination. From the courtyard, I closed my physical eyes and opened my inner eye to check for the presence of anything nonliving. I could feel several spirits nearby. Blocking their energy, I focused on the house in front of me. I could sense something, but I couldn't get a read on it from out here.

I opened my eyes to find Jesse leaning on the brick column on the porch waiting for me. "Hello." He pushed himself off the column at my greeting.

"Hello yourself." He kissed my forehead then linked his arm with mine to lead me inside. We walked thru the front door straight into the living room. Our footsteps echoed slightly on the laminate flooring. I could see the team had set up a base area at the kitchen table that was off the right side of the living room through an archway. One of Jesse's coworkers emerged from the hall that ran between the living room and kitchen. He was a giant of man at over six and half feet tall, salt and pepper hair, with a body that reflected his sedentary lifestyle under an ill-fitting grey suit. "Hey John. How you doing?"

"Holly." He barely acknowledged my greeting. Not really surprising. He was the team skeptic who was convinced all things paranormal were either overactive imagination or completely explainable by common sense. The rest of the team had started keeping track of how many times he told us that a creaking floor was never anything more than a loose joist. Being a nonbeliever, he was unwavering in his belief that Jesse and I were charlatans plain and simple. I could understand the need for a skeptic on investigations, I just didn't understand why we couldn't have a polite one or at least one that was nice to look at. Jesse gave him a hard look as he cut us off to enter the kitchen/dining room first.

"Yo Jesse's girl!" Paul, the team techy looked up from the laptop displaying all the cameras the team had been placing throughout the house. He was the complete opposite of John; young, obviously fit under his white slacks and lime green shirt, with blue eyes and short hair that matched his mocha-colored skin. He'd grown a fluffy beard since I'd last seen him. Growing up in a haunted house had made him a true believer. We bumped fists while I rolled my eyes. I'd trade Bush jokes for Rick Springfield ones. "We're all set up here. Are you ready to do you walk thru?"

Jesse and I both nodded. Paul and John went out the front door with Sara, the newest intern following behind them. Even though we could sense the house with the team in it, I had discovered that it was easier for me to develop a rapport with the spirits with fewer people around. Jesse didn't like me being in haunted places alone until we could establish what was there. If it was a negative entity, he could sometimes pick up on it sooner than I could.

I wandered into the kitchen which was not original to the house: stainless steel appliances that still had some of that blue protective wrap in the creases, metallic backsplash, marble countertop, modern looking cabinets. If they had recently done these renovations, they might have stirred up a former owner. For most homes it was the heart, where families gathered, the place where mom ruled her roost.

Not seeing anyone in the kitchen besides Jess, I headed out to the living area. The exterior wall housed a fireplace encased in painted white brick. The knickknacks scattered on the mantel and curio cabinets screamed old lady yet, the grey walls and white leather furniture screamed young modernists. I sent a silent prayer that I wasn't about to get drug into someone else's family feud. The house was beginning to have an eerie resemblance to my grandparents' with its mixture of old and new.

Jesse patiently trailed behind me when I went down the hall, keeping a sharp eye out for any signs that something was waiting to jump out and get me. I'd stopped trying to convince him I could walk a house without supervision after a deranged housewife had thrown me across the room in punishment for leaving a smudge on the bedroom mirror. She hadn't shown herself, so I was caught completely unaware. Jesse's gift would have allowed him to see her energy in the wall watching and known that she was not Casper the friendly ghost.

The hall ended at the door that led into the master suite. Once again, a mixture of traditional décor mixed with modern. The room was dominated by a wooden canopy bed, bulky matching furniture, but decorated with geometric designs in green and gold that clashed with the mauve carpet. The attached master suite looked as if it had been gutted recently and updated to the modern style; white and gold everywhere. Personally, I wasn't a fan.

"Are you getting anything?" Jesse asked from the doorway.

"The tingle running up my spine says there's been a female visitor recently. She hasn't shown herself yet. But it definitely feels catty." I let my eyes flit around the room, hoping to find something that would give me a clue. "You find anything?"

"There's energy all over the house. The kitchen seems to be the hottest spot so far." Jesse nodded back down the hall towards the kitchen. I slipped past him to go back down the hall; we needed to see what was down the other hall off the living room. We found two bedrooms and a bathroom. One bedroom was an office and the other a gym. Only thing interesting about the bathroom was that it was still decorated in the traditional manner. "What do you think? Mom and dad passed, now one of the children have moved in and updated it, causing mom or dad or both to return?"

Jesse shrugged. "Ready to call the team back in?" I shrugged back at him, and then headed for the front door. My husband followed like a trained puppy. "Don't even think about getting me a leash."

I sent him an amused look over my shoulder. Some would mistakenly think him being a psychic had let him read my mind. But I knew better. We'd been married for almost sixteen years, together eighteen. There were times we just knew what the other one was thinking. We found the rest of the team outside having a heated debate over moving objects.

"Trucks driving by can easily vibrate things off shelves; giving the impression they were thrown." John's pale face was starting to get red as he threw his hands up in frustration. I'd have sympathy for him being the only skeptic in the group if he would extend even the slightest bit of respect or curtesy towards the rest of us. "Why must you insist on saying it was a ghost?"

"Because sometimes things are thrown by unseen hands." Jesse's voice was sharper than normal. He didn't care for John either. After he told them we'd finished our side of things he headed back into the house. I watched him go inside then turned to John.

"I've seen a ghost cat bat around a glass bell until it got bored and knocked it to the floor." He narrowed his eyes at me. I smirked then went into the house where I found Jesse gazing at the knickknacks in the curio cabinet by the sliding back door. "Anything interesting?"

"Does that look familiar?" He pointed at a figurine of a young woman with pigtails, sitting on a white pedestal in blue capris and talking on the phone that was towards the back of the cabinet.

"I guess. It looks like all the other figurines from that era. Weird colors with creepy faces." I turned towards the door as it creaked open. Sara and Paul came in followed by a man who had to be in his late sixties and a woman who looked to be late thirties/early forties. John brought up the rear.

"Holly and Jesse Leefe, this is Michael Cook and his fiancé Libby Walker. They are the owners of the house." We shook hands. They were mismatched. Michael wore a tan cardigan over a brown shirt with khaki-colored pants. Libby was dressed in those active wear pants favored by woman today and a Taylor Swift t-shirt. He was almost bald while she had long curly hair dyed a grey color. But who was I to judge. I was in a black pantsuit with a hot pink shirt and heels. My husband was in a flannel button up over faded jeans with cowboy boots on his feet.

Libby ushered us to the couch where she began to tell us what had been happening in her home. Approximately six months ago she had moved in when they had gotten engaged. She'd noticed little things at first; the feeling of not being alone, doors that seemed to close on their own, what sounded like footsteps on the laminate. All things that could be explained away simply enough. She'd chalked it up to just needing to get used to living in an old house. A month or so later things started disappearing around the house, then reappearing somewhere else, sometimes days later. The activity had really cranked up when they gutted the kitchen. Objects went from just being placed elsewhere to being thrown around. One of Libby's stiletto heels had been thrown so hard it cracked the TV it hit. They replaced the tube TV with a fancy flat screen. They came home from work to find it had been pulled off the wall and lying face up on the floor, the screen cracked in a spider web pattern. That's when they stopped joking about maybe having a ghost and reached out to Jesse's firm for help.

The team had come out to investigate multiple times but had yet to obtain definite proof of a haunting. So far, they only had a few possible electronic voice phenomena caught on tape recorders plus spikes in the EMF around the house. John of course argued it was a combination of adjusting to an old house and the earthquakes that had recently been shaking the area. Since the team didn't actually see the TV, he believed it could simply have been mounted to the wall incorrectly and bounced off the hearth of the fireplace, causing it to land face up with the shattered screen.

Paul agreed that it was possibly nothing since they hadn't caught anything on film. However, he had brought Jesse and me in to be sure. Sara was convinced it had to be a ghost, because like, what else could it be? This was the first time I'd meet the kid. I'd been unaware that we had valley girls in the DFW area. Ignoring the gushing excitement that I could almost see rushing off the new intern, I turned to the homeowners. "Michael, did you notice any activate before Libby moved in?"

"Can't say I really did. It's just been me rattling around this old place for the past few years. A few times things weren't where I thought they should be, but my memory might be failing me." He answered, his words slow with a heavy Texan drawl.

"I feel confident in saying you do have a spirit hanging around. They unfortunately are not here right now." I paused to let them take that in. John released a deep sigh full of irritation. "Jesse and I don't live far from here, next time something happens call us. If we're here while they are active, I can talk to them."

Libby took the card I held out. There was a wobble in her voice when she spoke. "Could it be a demon?"

I looked at Jesse. His gifts would allow him to answer that better than I could. He put a comforting hand on her knee. "There's nothing here that feels demonic. I'm sure it's human. It doesn't feel negative either. I'd say it's more pissed off than anything."

"Did you find an anchor here?" Speculation colored my voice.

"There's something about that figurine, but it doesn't feel like an anchor." He pointed back towards the cabinet. I gave him a satisfied nod.

"You mind letting us in on the secret?" John was annoyed.

"That means they probably aren't a random spirit that you brought in the house because you bought their favorite pan at a garage sale. " I went on to explain that whoever they were, they were probably attached to one of the living in the house. Unless of course, they were a random neighborhood spook. That could happen. These houses weren't quite old enough for us to be really considering that yet, but it was a possibility. "I don't mean to be indelicate, but given your obvious age gap I have to ask, Michael, are you a widower?"

Faint sadness clouded his eyes for a moment before he answered. "I was married for almost forty-five years. She passed eight years ago. Car crash." Libby squeezed his hand. I hated dredging up painful pasts, but I needed to know if she was the vengeful type. He shook his head with a nostalgic smile. "She was the sweetest girl I ever knew. I know she moved on to where she's supposed to be."

With nothing else to convey, we began breaking down the equipment. It seemed wasteful to set all of it up when it was only in use for an hour and a half.

I took down the camera on the tripod in the home gym. Jesse followed behind me, rolling up the cords. He paused beside the rowing machine to look around. "Does this room feel wrong to you?"

"All home gyms feel wrong to me." I shook my head sadly. "What's the point of working out if you don't get to watch hot guys lifting heavy objects? Isn't that your reward for getting all sweaty?"

"I know a better reward for getting sweaty." A very naughty smile was on his face.

I dismissed him with a hand, keeping my head turned so he wouldn't see my smile. "Don't waste such an EWWWW inducing line when our offspring isn't around."

Shaking my head, I carried the camera and tripod down the hall to the kitchen. While I was putting the equipment in their foam lined cases, I heard John explaining to Libby and Michael how they had nothing to worry about. He was explaining his theory of how recent fracking had caused earthquakes which had knocked things over. It was my turn to be irritated.

I walked over to the trio. "You do realize we haven't had an earthquake for some time, right?" John glared at me as Jesse and I bade our goodbyes.

My husband escorted me to my Jeep. I put down the window after I fired her up. "The teams heading out for a drink. Wanna join?"

"Sure. Where?" Jesse named a bar in downtown Grapevine. We weren't big on bars, preferring each other's company to loud places that charged a fortune for a soda, we didn't join the team on their outings very often. But I could tell he really wanted to go. I had a feeling it had to do with multiple screens at the bar showing different games simultaneously.

"Be right behind ya." He leaned in for a kiss then stepped back to let me pull away from the curb.

4

Chapter 4

I didn't waste my time trying to parallel park in downtown Grapevine. Twenty some years ago I had failed that on the driving test and hadn't seen any reason to subject myself to that humiliation since. Especially with rows of windows that could be full of people staring at me. There was a parking lot across the train tracks where you parked like a normal person. On my trek to the bar, I texted the child to let her know we might be home after her. She had a yearbook meeting tonight. One of her girlfriends was supposed to be dropping her off.

Just as I walked in front of the bar, a maroon Austin Martin that still had dealer plates smoothly parallel parked in the tiny spot in front of the door. Wolf whistling, I clapped at the showoff. A striking tall honey blonde woman climbed out of the driver's seat dressed in a brown halter with giant pink dots flowed over faded jeans. She slid what I knew where designer sunglasses on her head while shooting me a look. Casual grace oozed off her as she strolled over to me.

"What? There's no men standing here to let you know you are hot." I flashed my most innocent smile.

"You are whistling at the car." Amusement snuck into her rebuke.

"You right. When do I get to play um, I mean drive it?" I couldn't keep the desire out of my voice.

"You can drive it when you grow up and can treat it like a vehicle and not a rocket ship." She chirped the alarm before dropping her keys in her bag.

Sadly, I shook my head, "So never then?" Violet slung an arm around my shoulders to pull me into boop my head with hers while we giggled.

"Are you following me?" I hooked my thumb towards the bar doors. As we walked to the double doors my best friend and confidant Violet Rose explained she had seen me pull in and stopped to see what I was up to.

"How did you know it was me? I'm not the only Jeep in town." Side by side we walked into the bar. No smoke rolled out to greet us. As a non-smoker I approved of the new no smoking laws. But non-smokey bars were just wrong. Sure, it was great to be able to carry my purse in and not have to through it out tomorrow because of the smoke embedded into the fibers, but I still found myself missing it. I paused as we stepped in. It had been redesigned since I was last here. The boring country bar I remember had been replaced with a gold and teal art deco look.

The floor was covered in tiny little square tiles, alternating white and teal. In the center of the room the stainless-steel bar had columns made of glittering teal, white, and black tiles. Teal wainscoting wrapped around it. Booze was on display inside gold ovals with a mirrored background. Long golden cylinders dangled from the ceiling with lights inside of them. Bravely they had padded teal barstools bolted to the floor. Golden tables filled the room. Each of them had a stained-glass light fixture above it with padded red chairs.

Vi and I exchanged glances before settling at a table that was out in the back corner but still had a decent view of the bar. We were surprised that the chairs seemed to be clean. Briefly I wondered how often they had to use an upholstery cleaner on them.

"You are the only neon purple Jeep with aqua trim and a tire cover with bigfoot carrying a lawn flamingo on it." Before I could come up with a witty retort, a waitress stopped by to ask what we were drinking. She gave us odd looks when we both ordered sodas before heading off to the bar.

"Any luck with house hunting?" I inquired while perusing the drink menu. Divorced and with both of her girls currently off at college at Texas A & M she was an empty nester. The family home was sold during the proceedings. For the moment she was residing in a luxury apartment in Frisco. Recently she had decided that she needed a McMasion. I had been accompanying her when I could to do a ghost check. Even though she knew a ghost could turn up at any moment, she wanted to make sure there wasn't anything attached to the home. So far she had only looked at new builds that were gorgeous but had no soul. Living or otherwise.

"I looked at a marvelous place in Highland Village. Five bedroom, five and three half bath. Multiple living spaces. Pool, Spa, outdoor living room. Game room and media room." Vi's eyes were starting to glaze as she listed the attributes of the manor. As an event organizer she threw tons of parties. Entertaining space was a must for her. "Are you going to be around this weekend to give a spiritual once over?"

"I'll have to check my schedule." Ghost hunting and parenting kept us way busier than I liked it. Hopefully I was free to go see what over the top lavish bachelorette pad she had her eye on.

The young waitress hadn't yet returned with our soft drinks when Jesse and Sara walked in together. We couldn't hear them, but Sara was looking up at my husband with a look that had me glancing at Vi to see if she saw it. We side eyed each other with a nod. They headed straight to the table. Jesse kissed the top of my head. The intern turned away, not watching us. We told them our drink order had been taken and they might want to go to the bar to order.

"Where's Paul and John?" I asked before they walked away.

"John's not coming, and Paul had to make a stop." Being a gentleman, Jesses motioned for Sara to precede him. She gave him a sunny smile as she sashayed in front of him. Vi and I leaned into each other as we watched them walk away. Sara was a cute little thing in her plain white tank top showing her white with roses bra and skinny fit jeans tucked into her red boots. They were both standing at the bar trying to get the bartenders attention when the waitress dropped off our drinks. The intern was standing closer to Jesse than was polite given their status. Her hand had somehow ended up on his. Jesse turned to look at her hand on his like he'd been grabbed by an alien.

"You going to do anything about that?" Vi asked.

"Nope. I'm going to watch the show." Being the evil person I was I sat back and took a long drag off the soda the waitress had just sat in front of me. Proving karma is real and a bitch, it was diet. With a face I swapped my drink with the one in front of Vi. She let out a laugh at my plight. "Three, two, on-"

First, I saw Jesse visibly pull his hand away and tuck it in his pocket while sucking in his stomach. I rolled my eyes. Such a guy reaction. Then he quickly grabbed the beer he had managed to order. He hightailed it away from the bar like it had shocked him. I was trying not to laugh. He scooted his chair close to mine before sitting down. He grabbed my hand that was resting on the table and laced our fingers. I couldn't say for sure, but his wedding ring was prominently displayed. The wanna be homewrecker silently dropped into the chair next to Vi. Brave of her.

I leaned over to whisper in my husband's ear. "Baby, I really need some cherries for my coke. You wanna be my hero by getting me some?" He looked at my sucked in lower lip and look that promised a sexy reward. I'm not sure his feet hit the ground before he got to the bar. With a smile I turned to the child at the table.

"You got good taste in men, honey. However, that one is mine. Look elsewhere." I nonchalantly sipped my drink. So much easier now that it was regular instead of diet.

"You sure?" She raised an eyebrow. The smug sureness of youth plastered on her face.

Vi and I both laughed. I threw up my hand to stop whatever Vi was going to say. "My name is tattooed on his soul. And other places come to think of it.' Vi and I laughed as Sara looked at us in disbelief. "Let me put this in terms you understand. You touch my husband again and I will put a poltergeist in your house. You cause him any trouble and I'll send the clingiest ghost I can find your way. If that's not enough to get you to understand he's off limits, I'll send you Carl. He likes to hang out in bathrooms and sit between you and the toilet seat. If you thought, there is nothing worse than a poltergeist keeping you up all night and a clingy soul that is always with you. Imagine never knowing if you were sitting on a toilet seat or a ghost's lap. To be clear, I'm not worried. Just annoyed."

"Tell what the tats are." Vi giggled. She was feeling evil obviously. Smirking I told the harlot. Jesse had the word Holly berries near his berries. Low on my pelvic area had the words Jesse's bush. The EWWWW was clear on her pretty young face. My BFF and I giggled at her discomfort.

Jesse returned then with a glass full of cherries. I grabbed his shirt to pull in for a kiss. "You rock my world."

Sara looked away in disgust. Stammering out an excuse she took her drink to the end of the bar where a guy that had been eyeing her since she walked in was sitting. Paul strolled in as Sara and her victim were heading towards the dance floor. Noticing we had drinks, he swung by the bar to get a drink.

Oozing charisma, he quickly charmed the waitress into handing him a bottle of a local IPA after bypassing the line. He paused to look at the napkin long enough, I suspected her number was on it. Even though his face was turned from me, I had no doubt he winked a flirty wink at her. Ill-gotten beer in hand, he sauntered back to the table. His blue twinkly eyes landed on every female in the room. They lingered on Vi.

Moments later he dropped into the seat Sara had abandoned. "Violet! Lovely to see as always. What brings you out tonight?"

Vi had been in Trophy Club on a date with her current boy toy. Since her husband ran off to California to sell his screenplay two years ago, she had been working her way through the most eligible bachelors of the Dallas metroplex. Vi giggled a little when Paul assured her his huge truck was just as luxurious as the boy toys Maserati.

"Men always bragging about how satisfying their "trucks" are." I popped a cherry in my mouth as the table snickered.

"It's refreshing to hear one that understands size matters." Vi and I clinked glasses. Her words were snarky but the eyes she sent him were flirty while sucking on her straw. There was starting to be tension here. A glance showed Jesse was side eyeing me. I pursed my lips and nodded. We didn't know which one to warn. Paul was definitely a lothario. But Vi was making up for all the lost time while she was trapped in a miserable marriage. This could provide entertainment from all sides. A few innuendos later Paul was leading Vi to the dance floor.

"That's going to be a catastrophe." Jesse took a drink of his beer. His eyes never leaving the couple engaged in a dance off to Bell Biv Davoe's Poison.

"Nah, it'll probably end badly." I injected while looking for the intern wanna turn mistress. She was currently in the corner playing with her victim's tie. If I was a nicer person, I might mention the two see through women talking smack about her. They were both in their late twenties, maybe early thirties. Judging from their skinny non-low-rise jeans I'd say they had only been deceased about five years give or take. A familial resemblance led me to assume the one in an emerald green leather jacket and gold sparkly cami was the sister of the victim. Bodily language had me suspecting the non-sibling in a coral halter top was probably the partner of the tie owner. I couldn't make out what they were saying but, I knew disapproval when I saw it. They paused their tirade when they realized I was looking at them and not the couple. I waved and smiled to let them know I was friendly.

They exchanged glances then did the creepy disappear and reappear beside our table. Jesse finally looked away from the dance off. Quickly looking his way, he nodded to indicate they weren't dangerous. I turned to them. "Ladies."

"Oh.My.God. You can see us!" The sister exclaimed in excitement. Both of them started to giggle. Up close I was fairly certain they had been killed in a car crash. Glass was embedded on their faces and arms. Non-sibling had a friction burn by her collar bone usually caused by a seat belt. Thankfully they weren't too bloody or icky. I gave a quick run down of me and Jesse. After the ohhh and awwwws they confirmed my car crash theory. Also, that the owner of the tie was in fact emerald jacket's brother and coral top was the girlfriend. This was the first time the brother, Brian had talked to another girl since they had died three years ago.

"Do you know that pick me?" The girlfriend, whose name turned out to be Clair lifted her chin in Sara's direction. I snorted before I filled them in on what I knew. Jesse stayed oddly quite during this exchange. After I filled them in, they wondered back over to explain in detail to Brian what a moron he was for talking to someone so desperate.

"You gotta keep Vi from breaking his heart. Do you know what happens when Paul is broken hearted? I have to watch all the footage because he's too busy trying to figure out what combination of flowers, candy, and jewelry will get her back. I can't do that again. His aura starts looking like rave lights. Gives me a freaking headache."

"She'll use him and cast him aside before his heart gets involved." I looked around for our waitress. My soda was nothing but ice. Remembering Vi's question from earlier I asked, "Do we have any plans for this weekend?"

5

C hapter 5
"Oh god yes. Oh yeah. Oh, that feels so good. MMMMM."
I moaned.

"Woman, you need to get to the doctor." The sound of my husband's voice had me turning to face him.

"Hmm?"I hoped my expression was innocent, which was a hard look to pull off with my hand cupping my ear.

"It's not normal to make sex noises while cleaning your ears!" He pulled the Q-Tip I was cleverly hiding inside my ear out of my hand.

"Concerned the Q-Tip satisfies me more than you?" The sweetness of my tone didn't match the challenge in my words.

He gave me a smug "please" look. "You've scratched your ears until they are swollen again, haven't you?"

"Nu uh." I'm sure my expression was petulant. Unfortunately, I couldn't focus on my expression while controlling the urge to scratch my ear canal.

"Go to the doctor!" Jesse grabbed the box of Q-Tip from the drawer. "You can have these back when you have a doctor's note."

I stuck my tongue out at his back. Once I was sure he was gone, I pulled a new box out of the linen closet beside the vanity. In the blink of an eye, the box was yanked out of my hands.

"I said get a doctor's note!" Jesse brandished the box at me before turning on his heel.

"Damn." I muttered under my breath. Ignoring the itch, I removed the little makeup I wore and put away my jewelry. With four cats in the house, if I wanted to keep it untangled and in pairs, I couldn't risk setting any of it on the counter even for a second. A brief stopover in the closet to change into clean pajamas from the hamper I'd shoved in there yesterday completed my transformation from professional woman to slob.

My fluffy pink unicorn slippers barely made a whisper as I crossed the tile in the living room on my way to the kitchen. I still had to make dinner. It was too late to make anything too in-depth. Looking in the pantry, I had half of everything I needed to make something. Perhaps I could talk my family into the baloney sandwiches we had missed out on last night. As I passed the stove to get to the fridge, I felt heat. I opened the oven with a hopeful look. Yes, someone had put some chicken strips in to bake.

SMACK. I whipped my head around to see who had dared spank me while I was bent over. Shocker, it was my hubby. "How dare you sir!"

"How dare me? How about how dare you be off molesting your ears instead of cooking dinner like a good woman? That's two nights in a row I've had to deal with dinner. Get naked." He had that wicked gleam in his eyes that I loved so much.

"EWWWW. There are minors in the room!" Savannah's voice sounded like she was in the dining room. Jesse winked at me. I stood up, gave him an affectionate smack to the breastplate, and then headed back to the pantry to see what I could make as a side dish. Score! There was a family sized mac and cheese hiding in the back.

"Why can't you buy the one with the creamy cheese? It's so much better." Savannah whined from the table. I never ceased to be amazed at how she knew what was going on around her without ever looking up from her screen. Judging from the lack of make-up and false lashes and that she was in her dancing coffee cup pajamas; I'd say she was in for the night. One of these days, I was going to have to start keeping up with her schedule.

"'Cause we ain't hoity toity folks. We eat powdered cheese in this house." My husband's East Texas accent was thicker than normal as he responded to our offspring. I high fived him before shooing them off to go feed the animals while I finished getting dinner ready. The kitten was driving me nuts circling my feet crying. Undoubtably there was still food in all the bowls, but the middle was probably empty causing the cats to be convinced they were going to starve. With the family off dealing with the critters, I was able to get dinner ready in peace.

"That's too much butter." My grandmother's voice over my shoulder startled me. I hadn't felt her arrive.

"Shit!" I shot her a dirty look before I stirred the hunk of butter I'd just scooped up into the pasta.

"Ladies do not use that kind of language. Put a dollar in the swear jar." She pointed at the jar on top of the fridge.

"That's Savannah's "I'm an entitled millennial jar", not a swear jar." I dumped the powdered cheese in and then poured milk on top.

"That's too much milk. It's going to be runny. The recipe is right there on the box. If you'd go to the cooking classes, you'd be able to follow it." Just what my night needs, a judgmental sous chef.

"Shouldn't you be off haunting the graveyard instead of criticizing my cooking?" I pulled the chicken out of the oven.

"That is not a balanced meal. You need a vegetable. You should make beets or brussel sprouts." She stuck her head through the fridge door. "Why don't you have any vegetables in here? This is all junk food." She made a disapproving sound. "Why are you letting my great granddaughter drink those silly energy drinks? Ladies do not walk around all jittery from caffeine."

"Those are mine. If you don't like what you see, might I suggest you go to the aforementioned graveyard?" The look I sent was definitely not respectful.

She pulled her head out of the fridge to give me a scathing look, and then looked into the freezer. "Why are you buying ice cream in pints? That's the most expensive. You need to buy it in the big tubs. It's much cheaper. Didn't your mother teach you anything about home economics?"

I bit my tongue to keep from telling her if she'd just cross over and stay there, I might not need Ben and Jerry as often. Well, I tried to bite my tongue. After she went down the moment on the lips, a lifetime on the hips route, with a pointed look at my mid-section, I mouthed off. We spent the next few minutes establishing that my tone was not acceptable and that I didn't care. As I plated dinner, I gave her the dreaded silent treatment.

"Fine. Be a pill. I'm going to go have a word with your mother about how she raised you." She disappeared through the garage door with a pseudo hurt sniff. Like magic, my family appeared just as she disappeared. I quickly texted my mother a warning that she had incoming.

"We scored that round eight to six, in favor of Eleanor." I tugged my husband's goatee as he passed me to grab his plate. "Careful, you're rather fond of that."

I rolled my eyes as we settled in for a quick dinner. The conversation wasn't as good as last night's. Instead of a brawl between coworkers, we discussed what we had felt at the house earlier.

"There was something off about that figurine. It's not an anchor." Jesse shook his head while dipping his chicken in sriracha sauce. "It has an energy attached to it."

"Ohhh. Maybe it was used in some kind of witchy ceremony! That would be so lit!" Savannah's eyes danced with excitement. My husband and I exchanged eye rolls at the new slang.

"You think they set it on fire during the ritual?" She shot her father a dirty look, not taking the bait.

Dipping my chicken in less fiery BBQ sauce, I pointed it at Jesse. "Could it have been used for a focusing object?"

"I didn't feel any of the energies I've encountered from those kinds of things. Could be some off shoot I've never felt. Or some amateur tried to do something." He paused to steal a piece of chicken from my plate, which I thwarted with my fork. "It wasn't a strong energy. More of residual.

Thump

We all looked towards the front door. Our neurotic Chihuahua/dachshund mix ran from under the table to the door barking and carrying on.

"Shut up Puck!" I ordered on my way to see who was knocking. It was a bit late for visitors. I looked back over my shoulder to my child. "There had better not be a cootie carrier out there."

Savannah squealed while fluffing her hair. Jesses' eyes slid to the door that led to the basement. With a flair, I threw open the door. A quick glance had me slamming it shut.

"Honey! We have a situation. I need a man!"

"I'm the only man you need." My husband strutted across the formal dining room to come to the aid of his damsel in distress.

"Ewwww! No. Bad parents! No flirting when your child is in the room." She paused. "No, no flirting ever!"

With a defiant look at my child, I used Jesse's beard to pull him to me and plant a loud kiss on him. The ew that elicited was extremely satisfying. The gleam in his eyes promised a good time later. He gave my ass a smack before opening the door. He too looked down and closed the door.

Thump, thump, thump.

"You need a man." My man told me.

I smacked his chest then pointed at the door. "I've got one. Now earn your keep."

Savannah came over to see what the fuss was about. She opened the door and screamed. On the front porch was our sweet little grey tabby, Luna throwing a dead mouse up in the air by the tail. She was such a tiny delicate girl we sometimes forgot that she had been a stray and was a prolific hunter. Thump. The mouse bounced off the door. It landed just inside the house with a splat.

Shooting my husband a displeased look, I pointed at the mouse, while making grunting mmmm noises. We'd been together long enough; he didn't need words to know what I wanted. He reached down to grab the mouse. Luna watched closely, her tail twitching slightly. Just before his hand could clasp around the tail, she darted in, grabbed the tail, and took off running into the front yard. She stopped on the front walk to throw the mouse in the air again while looking at us. Jesse once again went to grab the mouse and she darted off with it around the side of the house.

"At least it wasn't a boy." With a shrug, Jesse went back into the house. I nodded and followed him in the house. Dead mouse beat horny teenage boy every time. Savannah scoffed.

"Aren't we going to find Luna? We can't just leave her out her alone!" Worry tinged her tone.

"She'll be fine. It's not cold." Jesse gave a careless shrug. "She's got dinner."

He ran laughing into the house as a tiny version of him chased after him. Laughter from the drive caught my attention. Standing on the driveway was Grandpa Charlie, forever clad in his overalls and plaid button up shirt. He'd been gone for some time now, but I still found it odd to see him without his ball cap. It'd fallen off when he had his heart attack.

"Love seeing my girls so happy." He gave a wave before fading away. I smiled and waved towards where he had been. He never stuck around long. I shook my head and wondered if it was because Grandma Eleanor was always popping in. I could understand needing some time alone after sixty some years married to her.

I rejoined my family in the house to find them cleaning up the kitchen and dining room. We were debating what to have for dessert when my phone rang. "Hello?"

"Mrs. Leefe? This is Libby Walker. The cabinet doors in the kitchen keep opening and closing on their own!" She sounded more than a little freaked out. Can't say I blamed her; your first poltergeist experience was always startling. I assured her we would be right over.

"Mom? Please, can I go?" The hope glimmering in my daughter's eyes broke me. A quick glance to be sure her father agreed, then I nodded.

"Grab your stuff. We gotta go." I grabbed my flip flops by the back door. I might be willing to go out in PJs but, not house shoes. A girl had to draw a line somewhere.

"I just need to go do my make up." Savannah started for the bathroom.

"Nope. Go as god made you or not at all." Jesse called after her as he jammed his boots on his feet.

"Not even my eyes?" I snapped a picture of the horror on her face. That was definitely going to be my new lock screen. "MOM! I'm not wearing make-up. No pictures unless you are using a filter!"

"Get in the truck." Jesse rolled his eyes as he held the door for me and waved our offspring to hurry up. It was a short drive from Euless to Grapevine. At least mile wise. Savannah whined the whole trip about how embarrassing it would be if we ran into anyone she knew. I took the opportunity to text my mother an apology. As we pulled in front of the haunted house, my phone dinged with my mother asking what my child had done this time to have me apologizing for my teenage years. Since the occupants of the house were out in the courtyard looking terrified, I decided to fill her in later. The three of us jumped out of the truck as soon as Jesse got it into park.

I could tell there was a spirit nearby, but I couldn't discern anything about. Needing more information, I turned to Jesse. He was looking at the house with a frown. Savannah seemed excited, so whatever he was picking up, she wasn't. As a group, we walked up the drive where the residents met us. Michael looked like he was in shock while Libby's face was white with terror.

"I went in to make some dinner and then all of sudden the cabinet doors opened and then closed, over and over again. After I called you, the doors started doing it too. We ran out when the front door flew open." Everyone but Jesse jumped when the front door suddenly slammed shut. He'd probably felt an energy surge and knew something was going to happen. Weirdly, I hadn't noticed it had opened.

"You two stay out here. You too Savannah. Let us go check it out first." I held up a hand to cut off her objections. Jesse paused at the door to throw her a stern look before he preceded me into the house.

6

Chapter 6

The front door slammed shut behind us with a thud. I jumped. Jesse did not. His gaze was locked on the fireplace, which we started towards. We cleared the entry area, crossing into the living room area, then all hell broke loose. The throw pillows on the couch flew at our faces. We managed to block them. The magazines that followed them smacked us in the chest while we were distracted. I shot my husband an accusing look. His job was to make sure things like this didn't happen. Without taking his eyes off the fireplace, he shrugged. When we stepped further into the room, all the figurines in the curio cabinet turned and looked at us. That was definitely up there on the creepy meter.

"There's two spirits here." Jesse was scanning the area, I assumed to find the other spirit since he would feel the one standing in front of the fireplace that I could see. I squeezed his arm as I passed him to make first contact with our want to be poltergeist.

"Hello." The lady looked at me with surprise. I assumed she hadn't run into many people who could actually see her. "I'm Holly. This is my husband, Jesse. Who are you?"

The lady had to be at least seventy. Her hair was that red color that you could only get from using a rinse. Using the gold velvet track suit, I estimated her decade of death was the seventies, which meant this was not the deceased wife of Michael.

"Whoops." She muttered before diving into the fireplace. I turned to my husband to see if he could tell where she had gotten off to. Before he could answer, there was the whooshing of water from multiple directions. While Jesse darted into the kitchen, I veered off to the bathroom off the living room. All the faucets were running and the toilet was repeatedly flushing. The faucet at the sink turned off easily enough. However, when I leaned in to turn off the one in the tub, the shower came on full strength with icy cold water. The water should have been lukewarm at least. It was only October in Texas. Our water doesn't cool off until about December. Obviously, this ghost had a cruel streak. I could feel someone staring at me as I was ringing out my shirt the best I could in the shower.

"We're ghost hunting, not entering a wet t-shirt contest Woman." I shot a glare at my husband standing in the doorway. My startled shriek must have summoned him. "See what happens when you wonder off on your own?"

Proving my maturate level; I stuck my tongue out at him as I passed by. We followed the sound of running water into the master bath. Jesse turned off the shower without incident. When I reached for the sink taps, the cold water splattered me in the face. My loving husband snickered. I shot him the dirtiest look I could while cleaning my glasses off. "This is why I mismatch your socks when I put them up."

He dropped a kiss on the top of my head. Oh, like that was enough to get him forgiven. Ha! Without warning, he grabbed my hand and booked it to the kitchen. We rounded the corner into the dining room in time for me to catch a glimpse of an elderly lady in a fluffy aqua bathrobe disappearing into the wall into the side yard. I hadn't gotten a good enough look to be able to estimate her decade of death or any distinguishing details. Hopefully, Michael or Libby knew who had died in her bathrobe and might be looking to scare them. My spine wasn't tingling anymore, so I assumed the house was currently clear of the dead but not departed. Jesse nodded at my glance to confirm that his senses agreed with my spine. Hand in hand, we went out the front door to update the residents and our child.

"What happened in there?" Savanna's eyes were dancing. It was going to be hard to keep her out of haunted places much longer, which was a terrifying thought. She didn't have the sense yet to stay away from the bad places. Undoubtedly soon she would be bringing home a demon. Or worse, a clingy soul that just wanted to chat about how they ended up spending their afterlife wondering the earth. Those were impossible to get rid of nicely. At least a demon could be exorcised.

"Mild poltergeist activity. Nothing serious." Jesse looked back at the house in speculation before he continued. "I don't think they are trying to hurt you."

"They? We have more than one?" Libby seemed to pale further in front of our eyes. She grasped Michael's hand in a death grip. He grunted slightly. If I had to guess, I'd say she was digging those talons she called nails into him.

"I saw two. Both elderly. One had bright red hair and wore a gold tracksuit. The other had white hair and was in an aqua bathrobe. Either sound familiar?" Both of them shook their heads no. I let out a sigh. "I'd say this is personal."

Jesse nodded beside me. "They were both in visitation."

Savannah piped up to explain what her father meant. "That means they aren't earth bound and can pop down here for a visit anytime they want. So, they must be good ghosts."

Jesse and I both laughed. "No honey. That just means they can go wherever they want. Vengeful ghosts can still pop in if they want." My darling husband glanced at me. "Just ask your grandmother."

I snickered quickly before I could get my face back under control. Savannah rolled her eyes while muttering that Granny Eleanor wasn't evil.

Since the activity had stopped, we gathered around the kitchen table to go over what had happened tonight. Savannah listened with rapt attention to our description of our encounter. Libby and Michael sat in shocked silence. As I was telling my side of the story, Jesse went into the living room. He returned a moment later carrying the creepy figurine of the girl in blue capris with a rotary phone. Carefully, he placed it in the center of the table.

"What can you tell me about this?"

"They were my wife's. She got them as a child." Michael answered Jesse's question while looking at the creepy thing with a fond smile.

"Them?" Jesse and I exchanged a look. There was only one figurine like this in that case.

"There used to be two of them. The other one got broken. It just showed up one day on my night table. It fell off and shattered."

"I remember that! It was the first night I spent the night." Libby's fear seemed to have eased.

I held up a finger. "So, the first night you spent you here, a figurine that belonged to Michael, appeared in the bedroom and shattered?"

Michael and Libby nodded their heads to confirm that I had the order of events correct. Jesse spoke up then. "Do you have the pieces of the broken one?"

"I gathered all the pieces up and put it in a box in the garage. Didn't seem right to get rid of it. Norma Rae loved her figurines. Her mom got her those when they got their first telephone and she was always talking with her girlfriends. "Michael's voice took on a sad note as he spoke of his late wife. Libby once again patted his hand. He gave her a sweet smile. "I'll fetch those pieces for you."

Michael went through the door at the end of the kitchen and returned a moment later with a shoe box that had probably held women's sandals. Jesse kept his eyes on the box. Something glimmered in Savannah's eyes as she too looked at. Clearly the psychics were sensing something that as a medium, I couldn't. Carefully removing the lid, Michael revealed the shards.

Inside the box were the remains of what appeared to be a girl in yellow capris with pieces of a phone and pedestal. She was even creepier since her face had broken off in a chunk separate from her head and body. Jesse slid the remains to our daughter. "What do you feel?"

Savannah hesitantly took the face piece out of the box, running her hands over the whole piece. "It wants to be with its partner. It's sad that it's all alone in a box. Broken." Like the ceramic in her hand, her voice broke a little on that last word. I rubbed her shoulders as she handed the piece to her father. We all pretended we couldn't see the tears that welled up in her eyes.

The maturity she could show when using her gifts always amazed me. The majority of the time, she was a typical teenager full of slang that made no sense and worried about her makeup. Times like this, she could feel the pain of an inanimate object. I had never decided if that was better or worse than talking to invisible humans. She was growing up. Soon, we wouldn't be able to keep her from exploring her gifts on her own. Most likely, we had already passed that point and she just let us believe she stayed out of haunted houses. The child had no qualms about lying to our faces.

Jesse put the pieces back together the best he could and laid it beside the figurine in the center of the table. "Now it makes sense. Together, they are clearly an anchor." He looked at Michael. "I'd say you have had a spirit in this house for a long time."

"If it's an anchor, does that mean they are trapped here?" Michael seemed genuinely concerned for the welfare of the spirit. You didn't see that often in victims of a poltergeist haunting.

"It doesn't hold them here. It helps them find their way back." Pride beamed through me. Savannah had obviously been paying attention all these years.

"Why has it turned on us now?" Libby's voice quivered. Michael clasped her hands between his larger ones to stop them from trembling.

"It would seem that you, Libby, were some kind of catalyst. Perhaps they don't approve of your relationship. They might have been fond of Norma Rae or become attached to Michael and think of him as theirs. It could be as simple as they don't like the changes around here. Unfortunately, all we can do is speculating until we figure out who they are." I turned my attention to Michael. "Do you know where her mom got the figures from? If neither of the spirits are your wife's, then that might be our only clue if we can't get them to talk to us."

"Mary found them Dallas. I don't recall anyone ever saying where she bought them." I couldn't help but notice that Michael was running a finger over the intact figurine. He had clearly loved his wife. It broke my heart to think of him losing her when they should have had so many more years together. At least he had found happiness again with Libby.

"Is there a way for you to figure out who was selling them?" There was a catch in Libby's voice as she delicately wiped a tear from her eye.

"No. Too much time has passed. Trying to track something as innocuous as this would be impossible. Is Mary by chance still alive?"

TV has given people unrealistic expectations. I'm sure if my life were a TV show, some spunky blonde would jump on the computer and track down who was selling these figurines at the time Mary was in Dallas and discover they had belonged to their late mother who matched the description of one of the women I had seen and poof, mystery solved.

"No, she died in the mid-eighties. Frank, Norma's father, might know." Michael gave a sad shake of his head. "He's been in a home for years. Dementia. Mary has two sisters that are still with us. I can ask them if they know where she found them. "

"That would be helpful. We need to know if she bought them new or if she didn't, we really need to know where she found them. Anything can help."

"Whatever we can do to help." Libby sniffed as she spoke.

Since the spirits had left for the night, my family and I followed suit. No point having three ghost hunters in a house without ghosts. Tiredly, we crawled into Jesse's truck. Hopefully, the drive home would be more peaceful than the drive over had been.

7

Chapter 7
I had managed to score the early morning appointment at my doctor's office. My ears were itching, and Jesse had hidden all the Q-Tip. Even the ones in Savannah's bathroom. She had been savage this morning. Something about not being able to do her eyes right without them. Not wanting to deal with either of them, I made my Q-Tip with holding husband drop of the non-winged eye child on his way to work.

After checking in, I settled into the chair in the corner of the waiting room with a trashy magazine. None of the celebrities on the cover looked familiar to me. Briefly I wondered if I had become an old person. As I flipped through the glossy pages, a sheer form sat beside me. Carefully I glanced around to see if anyone was paying attention. No other patients were in the room and the staff were all on the phone.

"Hello Maggie." I slipped an earbud in my ear. God bless technology. In the old days people like me just looked like crazy people talking to themselves. Now I put on a headset or hold a phone up to my ear and talk freely. "Anything good going on today?"

She gave me a disappointed look. Maggie was quite the character. Based on appearance she had been a housewife in the sixties. With her brown hair in a bouffant style and her prim knee length skirt with matching jacket and pristine white gloves she definitely had that vibe. The first time I met her I had assumed she was prim and proper housewife who had probably died some mundane death. Nope she had been filming an adult film when the erotic suffocation had gone fatally wrong. There were still finger marks on her mostly see through throat. As cliché as it was, she had been a med school student earning money for tuition. Now she roamed medical locations.

"Mostly just allergies. Nothing good. I'm thinking about floating over to the ER." Maggie answered while looking at the glossy pages over my shoulder. She carefully studied each picture of male celebrities on the beach. "Not a hairy back in sight. Damn I was born in the wrong decade."

The wistfulness in her tone made me snort. "Men are still furry. They just wax now."

"I know! Dude I was haunting this waxing place down the road. You should hear them yell when they get their downstairs waxed.' She chortled while wiggling her finger at the page. I flipped to the next page that had the female celebs in their barely there bikinis. "My lingerie covered more than that. But at least I got to eat cheeseburgers."

We chatted while waiting for my name to be called. After about fifteen minutes a nurse opened the door to call my name. I told Maggie bye then pretended to end my "phone call". Strategically reading the warnings about smoking I managed to avoid seeing my weight when the nurse asked me to step on the judgy machine that thankfully now had a digital display. Listening to the old ones as the slid weight after weight was so demoralizing. Every thunk your self-esteem sunk a little lower.

In the room the nurse led me to I went over my ear itch issues. After she left, I pulled up Reddit to check out what kind of crazy drama people had going on today. Quickly I was sucked into the drama of just no in laws. When the doctor came in, I was disappointed since I hadn't found out what happened with the mother trying to bring both her husband and her boyfriend to her daughter's wedding.

"So, what did Jessie have to threaten you with this time?" That was how my doctor greeted me. Not hello or how are you. Instead of answering I stuck my tongue out at him. "I know you didn't come in voluntarily."

"He hid all the Q-Tips." I muttered with my head down in shame. While looking out of the corner of my eye I could see the humor light up his brown eyes. He chuckled while looking in my ears.

"Do you have a date for the charlatan gathering yet?" He was referring to the upcoming psychic convention that I was one of the main panelists of. Ten years back I had written a book detailing what it was like to see the dead. It had found quite the following. With its success my publisher wanted more. Now I have a successful series of books on being a medium and the dead that I have encountered. "Or do we need pull out the Ouija board to find out?"

"Ouija is for talking to the dead. For seeing the future, you need a crystal ball or tarot cards." I tilted my head back so he could check my glands. "Not to mention you might attract the attention of something you can't get rid of. A psychic STD if you will."

"Just what everyone needs. An invisible stalker." He washed his hands while he started explaining about what was causing the itch. Sounded mostly like blah blah blah to me. But yay there were ear drops that I could use to stop the itching. I just hoped Jessie believed me when I said it had to be applied with a Q-Tip. I had no idea where that man had hidden all the boxes. "Do you know who the MC is going to be yet?"

"They are trying to get Nathan Malcom to do it. They asked me to reach out to see if I can convince him." Nathan Malcom was an attractive goofy yet lovable actor that had made a name for himself years ago in sci fi shows. During one of the fight scenes on his space show a stunt had gone wrong and his heart actually stopped for a couple of minutes. During those moments he had a near death experience. Bright light, dead loved ones and even now years later, he can feel when the dead are close to him. We had gotten acquainted when I included his story in one of my books about near-death experiences. He and Jessie had also become friends who played poker anytime they could manage it. "He said he will if Jessie can beat him at some weird poker game."

"Strip poker?" We both laughed. I assured him I would have remembered that one. We talked for another few moments before he sent me on my way.

Eleanor was waiting for me in the car. I'd caught a glimpse of her through the window before I got to the car. I seriously considered getting an uber to work instead of getting in the car. It was way too early in the morning to deal with her drama. But since she knew where I worked and lived, she would track me down eventually. Mentally bracing myself I climbed into my Jeep.

"Good morning." I greeted my grandmother. Fixing a pleasant expression on my face I put the Jeep in first. Briefly I weighed the fun of holding the clutch a little longer than necessary to create a burn out to annoy her versus the lecture I'd get for doing so. Sighing, I pulled out of the parking lot silently and boringly. While I was being a mundane driver, she was making snide comments about how it was plebeian of me to use my gifts to sell books.

"You are insolent to parade yourself around these conventions." Her sour expression could have been used as inspiration for the next Disney evil queen. "Our family has always upheld the greatest dignity while helping the community. Now you are running around convention centers with actors and mystics!"

Arms crossed over her orange vest; disapproval wafted off her. Side eyeing her at a stop light I interrupted her tirade. "Did you really come here to lecture me?"

"Your mother has paint samples up in my salon." Based on my grandmother's description, it sounded like my parents were getting around to ripping out the avocado green wallpaper. She was angry with the light cheery colors they had painted in various places to test them out. "Paper is more elegant than paint. I held so many beautiful functions in that room. You need to convince your mother not to ruin my house. If I had known she had such poor taste, I would have left the estate to you."

"Granny, I'm not getting into this. Talk to her if you have an issue with what she's doing." No way was I getting in between these two. No point in mentioning that I wouldn't have moved to Colleyville. Jesse and I were perfectly happy in Euless.

"She's ripping out my gold cabinets! Can you believe she wants to replace them with pain white ones? My plush shag carpet is already ripped out. Ugly hardwood floors were laid last week. There is no warmth in that room now." She was looking at me with expectations shooting out of her eyes.

"Your will clearly left it to her. She is updating it. She gets to make it what she wants." I returned her glare. I didn't want to get caught between them yet, I couldn't seem to stop feeling like a monkey trapped between the cymbals.

"HMPH" With one last nasty look, she dissolved out of the passenger seat. Thanking God, I pulled into my parking spot at work. The dashboard showed I was only an hour late. Strange, I was sure it took longer than that just to drive from the doctor's office. Quickly I gathered up my stuff while wishing I'd swung by Dutch Bros for a coffee. A banana split frozen coffee would definitely hit the spot right now. Sadly, if I had given in to the urge, I'd have to listen to my spectral grandmother explain how ladies don't consume so much caffeine.

My heels clicked on the tile floor as I crossed the lobby to the elevator bay. A quick head nod to the receptionist on the phone was my only interaction. There were a few people scattered around the room on the fashionable yet, in my opinion ugly, black and white couches. I missed the red leather couches that we had before the owner started dating an interior designer. Thankful I didn't have a job that required me to have meetings, I pushed the button on the elevator. The silver doors slid open immediately. After I swiped my fob, it smoothly took me up to the third floor where my office was. It was Thursday. I just had to get through today and tomorrow then it was the weekend.

8

Chapter 8

Leaving late as usual, I was out of breath from my jog to my Jeep when I fired her up. The window of me being on time for dinner hadn't completely closed yet. Speed limits were only theatrical here in the Dallas 'burbs thankfully. Rubber was left behind as I cleared the parking lot. Once up on 114 I put on some Beastie Boys in the form of Sabotage to help keep my right foot down. I had twenty minutes to do a thirty-minute drive. Traffic Gods were in a very good mood. Close to on time I exited the highway for the side streets in Colleyville. Luck kept my brakes from screeching when I pulled in front of the imposing Georgian Revival styled house.

Red brick façade behind the centered white portico conveyed a classic elegance. White trimmed windows with the classic black shutters added a clean simple look. The nearly eight-foot white door with ornate moldings around it created a beautiful entry point. Once I slipped my heels off, I half jogged up the gleaming white sidewalk. As a child I used to swear it was never ending. As an out-of-shaped adult I had the same impression. During my hike I noticed mom had uprooted the begonias that my grandmother had lined the walk with and replaced them with a shrub in the shape of a gum drop. Couldn't help but wonder how loud Granny had shrieked over that. She loved her flowers. Leafy green plants had also replaced the rose bushes that used to line the portico. As I stepped under its cover, I glanced up to the balcony that ran around the second floor of the house. Rod iron flower boxes had been replaced with simple elegant white ones. The four columns that held the roof of the portico had been freshly painted. Someone had removed all the patio chairs that ran under the balcony.

Being family, I started to open the door to let myself in. Before I had barely turned the knob, my husband swung the door open while looking at his watch. Flipping him the bird I gave him a kiss on the cheek. "Thanks Jeeves."

"My lady." He bowed his head to me with an exaggerated gesture to enter the house. "I am humbled that a lady of your status would deem me worthy of your affection."

"I'll let you earn that affection later." I tugged on his goatee as I passed.

An impish gleam lit up his green eyes. "As you wish."

"Oh, farm boy." I called over my shoulder. Chuckling he offered me his arm. Happily, we walked down the mauve tiled hallway. It wouldn't have been so bad if the tile was only on the floor. Unfortunately, my grandmother had also lined the walls with a paper that was the same color with gold shot through it. Thick moldings with intricate carvings separated the paper from the copper tiled ceiling. Ominous dark wood doors lined the hallway. They were all seven foot tall with etchings. Secretly I hoped mom planned on replacing them. The expresso-colored stain on them never felt welcoming to me.

When my grandparents lived here the hallway was full of furniture and artwork. It was wide enough several people could walk side by side now that all that remained was a table with some family pictures surrounding a vase of blue sage. Jesse led me through the first doorway on the right. The double doors had been slid into their pockets, something I had always thought of as a magic trick in my younger years.

This was my first time in the parlor since my mother finished it. The plush mauve shag carpet was now a beautiful bamboo hardwood. Gone were the dark wood paneled walls. Highly textured stucco colored a burnt orangey/sienna color had replaced them. Plushy white fabric sofas with matching chairs were placed in the main part of the room. Accent pillows that matched the walls perfectly adorned them. Mom had replaced the open shelf bult-ins with floor to ceiling sage green cabinets with shaker doors on the bottom. The upper part was open, arching in the middle, with a few knick knacks. White wood blinds now filled the windows instead of the heavy black velvet curtains. The chandelier with dangling crystals had been replaced with a delicate silver one with twelve frosted glass lamp shades.

Looking around I noticed the room was empty. Raising an eyebrow, I looked at my husband. Did he by chance think we were going to have an interlude at my parents' house? Wouldn't be the first time, but I preferred a room more off the beaten path with a closed door.

"Savannah is fixing her face." He used finger quotation marks around fixing. "Jerry isn't home yet. Carolyn is in the kitchen. She said to wait here."

"Actually, I'm right behind you." All five feet two inches of my mother pushed a cute little drink cart into the room. The glass top shelf held a drink dispensing mason jar of lemonade and two silver insulated dispensers. The antique looking one with handles on either side held coffee. The bullet shaped one with legs dispensed hot chocolate. Sitting on a tray were seven mugs. The bottom shelf supported by two bicycle looking wheels held bottles of marshmallows, flavored syrups, creamers, and sugar.

"Mother, there's only five of us tonight." Mentally crossing my fingers that she had just brought spares and that she wasn't losing her mind. I did not want to deal with a medium with dementia. Not a pretty thing. Dad walked in right behind. I sighed with relief. If she went nutty, she was his problem not mine. He married her knowing how loony our family was, he must have been aware this could happen. Even after meeting my grandmother, he still married mom. I'd say he was crazy for that but, it's not like I won the mother-in-law lottery.

She shot me a cagey smile. "I can count dear." Dad gave her a quick kiss hello. Savannah ewwwed from the hallway. Apparently, all affection was gross to teenagers. Just hoped she had that feeling about teenage boys. Or any boys actually. Mom waved at the drinks. "Everyone help yourselves."

Savannah got there first. Filled her cup half with coffee. The other half was syrup, creamer, and sugar. Jesse muttered something about the vulgarity of it. Not sure if it was her ratios or the fact she used banana syrup and chocolate caramel creamer. He poured a cup of hot chocolate mixed in some s'mores syrup and the chocolate caramel creamer. Topped it with marshmallows then handed it to me. My eyes promised a dirty thank you later. Grinning, he poured a mug of lemonade which he added a dash of mango syrup to. Mom took it from him with a smile. Then he poured two mugs of plain coffee with no additives. One he handed to my dad. He kept the other then sat down beside me on the love seat.

Once everyone was settled with their drinks I noticed my mother's attire. Since retirement she was usually in yoga pants with a t-shirt and her hair in a ponytail. Tonight, she had donned a pair of khaki shorts with a cute little pink cardigan over a matching cami. Her shoulder length silver hair had been straightened. Pink teardrop earrings dangled from her ears. A hint of makeup was dusted across her face. Dad was in his usual jeans and polo. So that was no help. I decided to bite the bullet.

"Why you all gussied up?" The s'mores flavored hot chocolate tasted like ambrosia as I waited for my mother to answer my question.

"Javier and Jayme were supposed to be joining us. They just texted that they won't be able to tonight."

"Oh. That's too bad. Is everything ok?" When mom had started to renovate the house, she had hired Javier to help with the décor. He and his partner Jayme had quickly become friends with my parents.

"Everything is fine. Javi's latest client is having a breakdown over the bathroom tiles being more teal than turquoise." She laughed a little at her friend's predicament.

"What's the difference between teal and turquoise?" The cute little furrow appeared in Jesse's brow.

"About five letters give or take." I giggled at my joke. Everyone but my husband rolled their eyes. Pretty sure my daughter rolled hers hard enough I heard them. Jesse, however, gave me the your so cute look. Playfully I coyly batted my eyes at him. Savannah ewwwed again. Jesse and I high fived.

"Are those two still refusing to set a date?" When same sex marriage was legalized, they had immediately gotten engaged. During the planning their mothers had become overbearing. They tried to overrule each other multiple things. The couple reached their breaking point when they mothers called the bakery to change the wedding cake. Both of them. On different occasions. Now they refuse to wed until their mothers agree to behave themselves.

We sipped our drinks while updating everyone on the going ons in our lives. I was updating them on the dates of the upcoming book convention when the psychics in the room all looked at the credenza under the window like puppets on a string. Mom and I looked at each other in surprise when a ceramic cat figurine tumbled to the ground. We were the only ones in the room that could see the dead. However, my father, like my husband and child could see energy. "Looks like you got a poltergeist problem."

Mom gave a dry chuckle at my comments. "Mother has been driving me bonkers lately." I started to open my mouth, but she waved a hand at me. "I know. I'll find my balance and it will go away."

"If you want Granny, I can send you the link to the playlist I used to help when I manifested the 'geist." Savannah looked very earnest while sipping her banana flavored coffee. EWWWW. Mom graciously thanked her for her kindness. There was a moment of silence as we all thought back to the incident three years ago.

Swearing, I frantically stirred the pot on the stove. Why did all the recipes have to have a béchamel sauce these days? The flour just clumped in the butter. Adding in milk just made a clumpy flour island floating in a milky river. Scrolling through the recipe on my nook had no apparent relief. Why did they have to put their life stories on these things? I didn't give two flying forklifts about how they came up with it. Just tell me how to fix it!

"Uh, Mom?" Savannah's voice was hesitant. I looked up to find her standing beside the stove. Frowning I wondered how long she had been standing in there. Thankfully we had converted the swear jar to an entitled jar, so I didn't owe it money. "There's something in my room."

"Good or evil?" I asked as I tried to make the islands more of a marshland. Her response of um didn't help. "Ok, living or dead?"

"Ummmmm" She was looking at the floor. Oh, this couldn't be good. Rotating the knob, I killed the flame on the stove. Hurring, I went down the hall to her room. I threw her door open expecting to see some creature hovering in the corner. It looked normal in there. Posters mixed with pictures lined the pale rose pink and gray walls. The floor looked like her closet had exploded all over it. Her bed was unmade with half the bedding on the floor. Full sized cutout of some KPOP guy whose name always escaped me stood guard at the foot of the bed. Thankfully our neighbors lived far enough away they couldn't really see his outline through the window he was in front of. Not that I judged. A full-sized poster of Luke Perry graced my door when I was her age. Mom was startled many mornings by it. I looked at her questioningly. She pointed at the corner over her bed. "Can't you see it?"

Puck followed us in. He whimpered then ran away to cower in the hallway. Squinting hard, I focused on the spot she pointed to with my inner eye thrown full open. The faintest of black clouds became visible. It seemed to hover over the head of the bed. If my focus slipped at all, it disappeared. Oh joy. This could only mean one thing. "Anything you wanna tell mommy?"

"Like?" As she stood there looking at the floor, her discomfort was clear. For a moment I really looked at her. Thirteen years had passed so quickly. My little tomboy was gone. Now I had a girl that had learned how to use a straightener to make her blonde hair perfectly straight. Fake lashes that in my day we would have said they looked like RuPaul would wear them were almost on right. Today it's a compliment, we would have meant it as an insult. The dark not totally blended lines around her face said she had been doing some kind of contour or bronzer or something. I couldn't remember. According to her my makeup habits were from the dark ages. After those comments I always felt the need to check for lead in my rouge. Her little pink crop top left a strip of skin between its hem and the top of her black sweatpants. At least she was bare foot instead of in heels.

"Honey, that's an emotional poltergeist. Kids hitting puberty can generate them. Especially gifted girls." I tucked a hair behind her ear. When had she gotten a third hole pierced? Tabling that for now I put it in terms she could understand. "The big red light on the console is going off. There's a wrecking ball working its way through your brain right now."

"Inside Out? Really mom?" Close to straight lined smokey green eyes rolled at me. We both turned when we heard heavy booted feet running down the hall towards us. Jesse barged through the door. His eyes darting around. Quickly he found the dark cloud on the ceiling. Us girls just looked at him. Loathing clear on his face he pointed at it.

"Is that what I think it is?"

"Proof that our little girl is becoming a woman? Yes. Yes, it is darling." I swear I saw him swallow. The fear on his face was hilarious. Knowingly I looked at my child. "Do you wanna talk to me or him?"

Jesse backed up two steps. Green eyes flicked towards the basement door. "Mom. Definitely mom."

My coward of a husband ran out the door straight to the basement. He didn't even pause to make sure the door closed behind him. Puck's claws clicked down the stairs. I sat down on the messy bed. When I leaned over to untangle the sheet from my feet our dog S'mores took the opportunity to lick me from hairline to jawline. We'd taken him in six months ago when he turned up as a stray at my in laws place. Everyone feared the poor guy had been dumped since he had house dog manners yet, no one claimed him. Savannah named him once we noticed he was mostly black with tan accents and a white spot on his chest. Not sure if he followed us like Puck or if he'd been hiding in the debris that was my child's room. The disturbance didn't seem to have any impact on him. Child like laughter had me looking at my half-grown child. I patted the bed. "What's going on?"

From beside me I heard muttering noises. She was so much like her father. Change of tactics might be needed. "What does it look like to you?"

She shuddered then described it from the viewpoint of a psychic. It was inky black floating over the bed, oozing down the walls from multiple locations. undulating to a staticky noise that it produced. My turn to shudder. "Baby, we can make it go away. But you gotta talk to me. Is there perhaps a boy that's caught your eye?"

"MOM!" I threatened to tell her about my first manifest. She started babbling then. There was a new boy at school. He was six foot tall with black hair and the bluest eyes ever. He smiled just for her. God, I hoped I hadn't sounded that sappy when I went through the same thing at her age. "When I dropped my book, he picked it up for me."

"Awww. What a gentleman."

"We're going to get married someday." Couldn't help but wonder if Jesse had thought to build a dungeon in the basement. After she waxed on about how perfect he would look in a tux I had her check out the poltergeist. "It's not oozing as much!"

"You're dealing with your emotions. Keep a diary. Channel everything into it. If you let it build up again, it'll get bigger. Stronger. This is a baby one. It'd be a shame if it got so big it could move things around and trash your room." I waved my hand around to indicate all the mess on the floor. She giggled as intended. I kissed the top of her head and went to see if my bechamel could be saved. Also wondered if my dome lasagna really needed it.

A timer going off in the distance brought me back to the present.

"Dinner's ready. Grab your drinks." Mom jumped to her feet with her lemonade. The rest of us followed her down the mauve hall to the dining room that was two doors down. The smell of stir fry filled the air when the door was opened. Yummy.

9

Chapter 9

Sprawled out on the plush leather chaise in the corner of my office, I swore at my phone. Thanks to a text from the hubby, I missed my shot at the eight ball.

"Call me" That was the message so important it might cost me the game. He'd gotten me hooked on this game months ago when it was easy to get the rings, just had to win so many games and poof you had a ring. Then they changed to a trophy system. Win get trophies, lose they took them away. Getting a ring now was like trying to pay off a high interest credit card by only making minimum payments. I'd been trying to get my champion ring in Jakarta for a month. Two more wins to victory. If he cost me this game, he wasn't going to like what I called him. Seconds later, my opponent potted the eight ball and now I needed three wins to get my ring. With a growl, my finger punched the button to call hubby dearest.

"You cost me my Jakarta ring." My tone no doubt conveyed that I was unhappy, and he was going to pay for his interference.

"Like those are hard to get. I've got two." Apparently, I hadn't married an intelligent man. What did that say about me that it took me almost twenty years to figure that out?

"No, you don't. You have one." I knew that for a fact, I'd just stalked his profile to make sure I still had more rings total than him. He gave a knowing snicker.

"I got a call from Mrs. Myer-Hutton."

That name mixed with his taunting tone made my teeth snap together. It was pointless to ask but, I had to try. "So, you are going to be late for dinner?"

An evil chuckle came across my phone. "No baby, YOU are going to be late for dinner. You know she thinks I'm useless."

"But she likes you more!" We went back and forth for a few more minutes before I accepted my fate.

"Fine! I'll deal with the old bat. You better have a decent dinner waiting for me. "

"I'll buy you a burger or nachos. If you are a really good girl, I'll even buy you a drink." The amusement in his tone meant I had forgotten something. I pulled the phone away from my face and the date made me swear again. "See you tonight Beautiful."

He hung up before I could talk my way out of going anywhere tonight. Man, my lunch break had been being so relaxing. Nothing like a call from the ball and chain to ruin it. Grumpily I returned to my desk and lost myself in work until it was time to leave for my evening of torture.

After fighting traffic for over an hour I pulled up in front of a Tudor style house in Keller. I hated this house. Don't get me wrong, it was gorgeous. It had the steep gabled roof and elaborate windows and doors that made it look like it belonged in the English countryside. It was the nutty old bat that owned it that had me looking for comfort in a frozen coffee from Dutch Bros and scone from Starbucks. Her hearing was obviously still keen; she opened the heavy wooden front door to stare at me as I washed the last bite down. I sent a fervent prayer for patience skyward and got out of the jeep with a smile.

"Good evening Mrs. Myer-Hutton." The woman had to be at least seventy. Her nearly shoulder length white hair was perfectly styled for a fifty's movie. Her lime sparkly pantsuit whispered as she raised her arm to look at the fancy gold watch on her wrist.

"You are late. Your darling husband said you would be here nearly twenty minutes ago." She admonished me in a sharp tone full of accusation. So, it begins.

"I apologize. Starbucks had a long line." Since she was a client of Jesse's firm, I had to try to maintain a level of professionalism. She sneered when I said Starbucks. Not sure what her problem with it was, didn't care. "So, what's been happening around here?"

Without speaking, she led me through the sparsely decorated entryway then turned left into the parlor and gestured for me to sit in the antique club chair. I swear she brought me in here because she knew the paintings on the wall creeped me out. They were poorly drawn portraits of her family members that she had made herself over the years. Either she couldn't draw, or all of her family had lopsided eyes.

"The activity started exactly nine days ago." She looked towards the door that led to the kitchen as she launched into her tale.

Nine days ago, was her sixtieth wedding anniversary. She went into the kitchen to make her anniversary breakfast consisting of eggs benedict served on Belgium waffles. While pouring the batter onto the iron, she felt a cold breath on the back of her neck. Startled, she spun around to see nothing behind her. When the waffles were cooking, she began making the sauce for the eggs. Everything was normal until she turned on the blender. The top flew off the top causing the blender to overflow onto the counter. Simultaneously, all the lights flickered in the kitchen.

"Lenny?" She called out hoping her beloved late husband was visiting her on their anniversary. There was no response. Unnerved, she returned to preparing her breakfast, feeling eyes watching her from the nook. Once the food was ready, she carried her meal to the formal dining room where she and Lenny had always taken their anniversary meals. Lenny's chair at the head of the dark heavy table felt cooler than normal. Again, she called out for Lenny with no response. Wondering if she was losing her mind, she settled at the table to eat her eggs with Nat King Cole playing on the record player, just as she had ever since Lenny had died nearly ten years ago.

Not wanting to focus on the odd incidents, she spent the day out with her daughter and grandkids. That night when she returned, the door flew open when she unlocked it. "Hello?"

There was no response to her greeting. Clumsily, she closed and locked the door. On edge, she hurried to her room. Halfway up the steps, she heard footsteps behind her. Every step she took, someone took one behind her. She whirled around to see who was in her house. Nothing was behind her. Even more uncomfortable than before, she took the remaining steps to the hall as fast as she could. The footsteps sounded like they were right behind her now. As quickly as she could, she dashed down the hall to her room, slamming her bedroom door behind her. There was a thud as if someone had hit the door. Frantic, she grabbed her bible from the nightstand and began reciting Psalms. Silence filled the house. She laid in bed the rest of the night, afraid to close her eyes, praying for daylight.

Over the next few days, she felt cold spots where Lenny liked to sit. Then she started hearing voices in the rooms on the back of the house on the ground floor. It sounded as if a man was whispering in her ear. Again, she was convinced it had to be Lenny. He would always sneak out the back doors to hide while smoking a forbidden cigar. She gave a sad shake of her head. "Blasted cigars is what killed him. If he had just listened to his doctor, he could celebrate our anniversaries with me without scaring me half to death!"

I gave a polite nod and she returned to her story. Wanting to know what Lenny was trying so hard to tell her, she went out and bought a digital recorder. A silent groan escaped me. No. Not EVP's. Electronic Voice Phenomenon or as I called it Everyone Vants Phantoms. "EVPs are not that reliable Mrs. Meyer-Hutton."

"Maybe not for you!" Her brown eyes flashed fire at me. "I know what I heard."

She pulled the recorder out of the drawer of an ancient-looking end table beside her far more comfortable looking Queen Ann sofa she was sitting on. I shifted in my chair. The cushion had probably flattened out decades ago. I swore she always made me sit here out of spite. "Listen."

She pushed the button on the recorder. There was the expected static. Occasionally what sounded like it might be a voice but, I couldn't make out any words. "What do you have to say for yourself now?"

Somehow, I managed to put on my polite and professional smile. "What do you hear?"

There was a superior gleam in her brown eyes that complemented the sneer in her voice. "Clearly it is Lenny telling me that he loves me and he will miss me while he is gone. Surely you can hear that! You are a physic."

The irritated sigh I'd been holding in escaped. "I am a medium. Not a psychic. I can see and hear the dead. IF there were any ghostly voices on there, I would hear it just as clear as I hear you. That is nothing but noise." Her mouth dropped open. I was usually nicer to her. More gently I continued. "You miss Lenny. You want to hear his voice again. But he has crossed over. He's where he is supposed to be."

"How do you explain the voices? The cold spots? The footsteps?" She was growing agitated.

I'd investigated this house on multiple occasions. The first time Jesse had been with me. Neither of us had sensed any paranormal activity. I had never sensed anything on subsequent visits. "You said nine days ago?" Her nod was barely perceivable. "We had a cool front come through. Your heater probably kicked on."

If my memory served, there was an air vent in the kitchen where she was probably making breakfast. There was another one by the dining room table. The cold spots and breath could easily have been caused by the frigid air being pushed out of the vents. I figured the footsteps had just been her own echoing and since she was already on edge, they scared her. Since the voices were only in the back of the house, I suggested they might be her neighbors. The lots here were so small they might as well be zero lots.

"What about the flickering lights young lady? How do you explain those?" She was becoming agitated. Just once I'd like to come here and tell her she didn't have a ghost problem without it becoming hostile.

"Get your wiring checked. You could have a short."

"There is nothing wrong with my wiring!" She jumped up, pointing a finger at me. Fine. She wanted to escalate, so would I. I jumped up and pointed a finger at her.

"I highly doubt that!" Biting back the urge to tell her what was wrong with her wiring. I continued in a more professional tone. "The house is from the fifties! You need to have it checked. It might still be the knob wiring in here! You need to check the plumbing too."

"You are always so impertinent! You know the way out." She flicked the finger that was pointing at me towards the door.

"A pleasure, as always Kitty." I said on my way out the door.

Through the door I heard her yell "It's Kathrine!"

I giggled all the way to my Jeep. I know it was wrong to taunt her, but this was my fourth trip here in six months. It was my turn to yell when I got in.

"You really should show more respect to your elders." Grandma Eleanor was in the passenger seat. I stared at her in disbelief. She had refused to deal with batty old women like Kitty when she was alive. She had no patience for those that wanted to be haunted and only worked with people that she felt deserved her help. "Have you spoken to your mother?"

"Talk to her all the time." I received a dirty look for my flippant tone. When it became clear I wasn't going to say anything else, she sighed.

"Has she told you what she is thinking of doing to my sewing room?" Her voice was heavily colored with disapproval mixed with exasperation. Uh oh. Things were about to get really ugly. I decided my best avenue was to play ignorant.

"She hasn't mentioned anything specific." I put the Jeep in first and resisted the urge to peel out as I pulled away from the gingerbread house that contained a nut.

"She wants to turn it into a yoga room! I didn't raise her to be so hippy dippy. She wants to put a Zen fountain in there! What will people think?" The horror in tone was almost funny. She had never worried about how her behavior affected us. But boy howdy, don't let anything we did make her look bad amongst her old biddy friends.

"Granny, it's her house now. She can do whatever she wants with it so long as daddy agrees. Besides, yoga is good for our kind. Helps keep our minds clear." I knew I'd misspoken when her eyes iced over. Damnit! She'd managed to drag me into the fight!

"No one ever takes my side. It would be nice if just once, one of you stuck up for me and what I want." With a pathetic sounding sniff, she disappeared from my passenger seat. I texted mom while trying to keep the car in my lane. Once she was warned that she was being spied on, I texted Jesse to let him know I'd left my hell and was on my way to meet him and our offspring.

10

Chapter 10

On the third circle of the tiny parking lot, I decided to park in the weird triangle shaped spot beside the median that jutted out. My Jeep fit perfectly once I put two tires on the curb. Not wanting to be tortured just yet, I loaded my pool game. Moments later I was lining up my shot on the eight ball. I was about to be two games away from my ring. My finger was sliding the doohickey to choose how much force to use. I sucked my lip between my teeth.

Jason Aldean's A Girl Like You suddenly filled the car and my husband's face was on my screen.

"Why do you hate me?" Perhaps not the friendliest greeting for my spouse but, he'd now knocked me back to four games to get my ring.

"Stop hiding in the car and get in here." Not even a little remorseful. He was so lucky he was hot. "Do you have cash on you?"

"Of course I don't have cash. The guy I do private dances for only uses credit." I grabbed my wallet out of my bag before shoving it under the passenger seat. "Doesn't even tip. Which seems unfair given the filthy things he asks for."

"Oh, I'm sure he gives you more than just a tip." I could hear Savannah's ewww in the background. With a giggle, I beeped the car alarm. "See you in a few."

A few minutes later I reached the opening in the chain link fence. There were a surprising number of police officers standing guard, mingling with the school security people. Two officers were working the entrance table. Now I understood why I needed cash. There wasn't a card reader in sight. According to the sign I needed seven bucks to get in. I shook my wallet. There were definitely some coins in there. Doubtful that there was seven dollars' worth of quarters. Maybe I could pass for a student. They only need five dollars.

"Don't try it. You can't pass for a college senior let alone a high school one." A warm shiver went down my back as I felt warm arms wrap around my waist. I didn't even question how he had managed to sneak around behind me.

"You calling me old?" I snuggled my head into his chest as we waited to pay my entrance fee.

"You think I'm going to walk into that trap, woman?" I could feel him shake his head as his arm reached out to pay the officer to the left of us. She stamped my hand then waved us on when she saw the stamp on Jesse. "Come on, you have already managed to miss the first half."

We strolled over to the bleachers hand in hand. I looked up into the stands to see our daughter sitting almost perfectly center. Wonder what time they had to get here to get those kinds of seats? Minutes later, we were all settled on the padded stadium seats that Jesse had insisted on buying the summer before Savannah started high school. He had been convinced that we would be spending every Friday night watching football. He'd grown up in East Texas where Friday nights in the fall equals football. Even if you weren't still in school or if you didn't have a kid at the school, the whole town gathered at the game. Sadly, he had failed to take into account how much our child hated football. She had refused to come to any game. He'd tried to convince me to come with him. Silly boy. I didn't want to spend my Friday night out in the heat or cold depending on how the Texas weather was swinging that night. So, the poor guy spent a bunch of money on seats a year ago that had never been used.

Then our daughter met Jock Boy. A six foot three two-hundred-pound linebacker with a smooth deep voice that knew how to bewitch a teenage girl. On more than one occasion, I had heard my child waxing longingly with her friends about his caramel-colored skin with his brown eyes that seemed to glow. I didn't trust this boy one bit. We had made it to sophomore year without her having a serious boyfriend. Personally, I was hoping to get her out of high school before she started dating.

Jesse handed me what I assumed was a burger wrapped in foil and slid a box of fries into my lap. "Is it edible?"

"Yes. Journey's dad makes them." Savannah answered without taking her eyes off Jock Boy on the sidelines. My mouth watered as I unwrapped the burger. Journey's dad owned the best BBQ joint in town. I knew my taste buds were in for a treat. "Why isn't he playing?"

"Uh because he's defense and the offense is on the field." Jesse answered without taking his eyes off the field. Jock Boy chose that moment to look up into the stands. I could tell from the flirty smile that he had found my little girl. I wanted to throw my fries at him. But that was probably against the rules plus a waste of good food.

After I devoured my meal, Jesse gathered up the trash and claimed he was going to throw it away. He looked offended when I scoffed at him. Clearly, he thought I was blinded and didn't notice the group of dads gathering over in the grass. He wasn't going to be back for a while. He played poker with about half of them. Savannah watched her dad carefully walk down the bleachers.

"Mom?" She leaned close to whisper in my ear. I tilted my head to let her know she had my attention. "What's a first down and how can we have more than one per game?"

I snorted soda out of my nose. This child came from a football family. There had been brawls on Thanksgiving. My family were die hard Chiefs fans. My husband loved his cowboys. There were a few traitors in the extended family that had been swayed by the dark side. One year a traitorous distant cousin who showed his lack of intelligence by rooting for the Cowboys over the Chiefs was dangled off the second-floor balcony at my grandparents. Sadly, we had to pull him back up before we got him fully extended out of fear that one of the adults in the living room below us would see his feet dangling in the window.

As quietly as I could I explained the rules of football. Every play she had a question. Finally, she just looked at me and waited. As the evening progressed it cooled off. We snuggled under the blanket the man of our house had thought to bring. In what felt like a blink, we were to the two-minute warning, which I had to explain. Since we were getting our butts kicked out there, there was no chance of us going into overtime. As much as I loved having my daughter's attention, I wanted to get home where there was central heat.

The sound of the final buzzer had everyone on their feet to applaud the effort of the boys. They rarely won a game, but they always played hard. I gathered up our things while Savannah giggled with a gaggle of girls. Judging by the sideways looks they were casting towards the field; I'd put money on that they were talking about football players' butts.

Once all of our gear was gathered, we slowly made our way down the metal steps to the main aisle. The slow pace was only partially due to my heels and mostly because my offspring felt the need to stop and speak to everyone she knew. About halfway down I was wishing for a more socially awkward child. At this speed, there was a chance I was going to run into other mothers. Like most predators, the more of them together, the more dangerous they were. I hadn't been welcomed by the mothers at any of the schools. They all knew I "saw" dead people. There was a large stack of cards for psychiatrists at home that I had been given by other parents. They thought I was delusional. I had never decided if that was better or worse than the ones that thought it was cool I could see the dead and wanted me to contact someone for them. They were never happy when I explained summoning the dead was a bad idea. Anyone with any brains knew better than to open that door. Unfairly, they all accepted Jesse and his gifts. Thought he was all new agey and cool or so they said. I was convinced it was because he was attractive and an involved father.

Finally, we reached the main aisle.

"I'll catch up with you." Savannah waved me off as she veered over to a gaggle of teenage girls leaning over the railing talking to Jock Boy. Shaking my head, I carefully went down the metal steps, mentally crossing my fingers I wouldn't hook a heel on them and do a face plant. Safely on solid ground, I went in search of my missing husband. The pack of fathers had moved from the grassy area they had been in earlier. I figured they had migrated to the concessions stand. Journey's dad most likely had his smoker there. Knowing men as I do, they tend to congregate near outdoor stoves even if they avoid the indoor ones like the tampon aisle.

I reached the point where the sidewalk split to form a circle around the grassy area that had the flags and memorial bench for the football coach that died a few years back. There were parents huddled in groups on either side of the circle. Not wanting to risk the catty ones, I slipped my heels off and jogged across the grass. On the way I nodded at the coach sitting on his bench.

Safely on the other side of the loop, I followed the sound of male voices to parking area behind the cinder block building. I rolled my eyes when I finally could hear their conversation. They were discussing the best dry rub ingredients. I made a mental note to mention this the next time he made fun of my friends and me for anything.

Meanwhile at the Cook/Walker house

Libby pulled her 2023 Land Rover into the middle of the garage. Michael had started parking his old sedan in the drive to prevent the Rover from getting dings. She carefully opened the door, making sure it didn't touch any of the junk she had moved out here when she moved in. On the left side of the garage is what Libby assumed an old ladies wet dream looked like, mostly old furniture and porcelain knickknacks. She walked around the vehicle to the rear hatch to unload her finds. Not wanting to make multiple trips, she rolled the little black shopping cart that Norma Rae had used to haul groceries into the house. Libby didn't buy enough groceries to ever need it for that. However, a day spent at Legacy West in Plano had given her a trunk full of shoes and other bags that could fit. While loading the shoes into the bottom of the cart, she felt eyes on her. Poking her head around the car, she expected to see Michael coming to help her. Seeing no one there, she turned in a circle, looking for anyone.

"I'm losing my mind. Stupid ghost." Libby muttered under her breath as continued loading her bags. She had grown to hate this house. Every room felt like there was already someone in there and she wasn't welcomed to join them. Her favorite stiletto heel had been used to break the old TV. She didn't object to upgrading to the Sixty-five-inch flat screen. Her objection was that the ghost had used her nude Louboutin. The heel broke and she had to go buy a new pair. Her bags filled the cart causing her to have to carefully tilt it so the rest could balance on the handle. Slowly she rolled the cart to the front passenger door to retrieve her giant handbag with the golden MK on it.

The slight step into the house rattled the cart. Libby swore under her breath, hoping Michael wouldn't hear. He was always reminding her that ladies didn't use such language. She liked his old fashion manners, but wished he had a little more updated vocabulary. Thankfully he didn't know anything about designer clothes, so he had no idea how much money was in the little cart. The garage door rattled down after she pushed the button that looked like a doorbell by the door. After the deadbolt was thrown, she moved into the main part of the house.

"Baby I'm home!" She called out as she rolled the cart down the hall to the master bedroom. The bedroom was closed. *That's odd.* They never closed the door during the day. The doorknob wouldn't turn under her hand. She tried turning it the either way. It wouldn't budge. Finally, she knocked. "Baby are you in there?"

There was no response from the other side. Frustrated, she kicked the door. It swung open easily. Sighing with frustration she rolled the cart inside to the master closet. "Stupid old house. Doors never stuck in my townhouse."

Joyfully, she began arranging her new shoes into the custom shoe rack Michael had installed for her. It ran the width of the longest wall of the master closet. Once she was satisfied with her shoes, she moved to hang her new clothes on the opposite wall. To make them fit, she had to remove some of her summer clothes. Those would have to be hung in her overflow closet in the office. Libby still felt like she was being watched. Michael was obviously not in the house. He had probably gone for his evening walk around the neighborhood. A chill ran down her spine as the laminate floor creaked behind her. She felt her breathing speed up. The feeling that someone was standing right behind her was triggering her freeze response.

"There's no one there. Just turn around and look." She muttered to herself. With a steading breath, she slowly turned around.

The closet was empty except for her. Quickly she gathered up her summer clothes. Still feeling the effects of the adrenaline rush, she all but ran across the living room to the office. The closet door opened slowly with a creak. Telling herself it was opening because of her stepping on the wood floor, she hung the clothes in her arms and fled the room to the kitchen.

"It's just your imagination." She tried to ignore the heavy steps that seemed to mimic the softer clink her red bottom shoes made. In the kitchen she made a light dinner salad from kale which she took along with a bottle of mineral water to the living room. Once settled on the couch, she turned on the sixty-five inch TV they had bought to replace the one that had been pulled of the wall to watch The Real Housewives of The OC. She had only watched for a few minutes when she began hearing a thunking noise from the master bedroom. At first, she tried to ignore it. The psychic said that the ghosts weren't there to hurt them. So even if she wasn't imagining it, there was no danger. She went back to watch her show.

Halfway through the episode the scratching sound of something sliding across laminate pulled her attention from the TV. With trepidation, Libby carefully sat down her salad bowl to pick up the metal object that had bumped against the couch leg. It was a gold MK insignia. Furious, she jumped to her feet and ran to the master bedroom, bouncing off the door when it slammed in her face. She took a step back to rub her forehead. The door creaked open slowly again. For a moment, Libby thought she heard a female snicker. When the door was fully open, she darted into the master closet.

Expletives rolled off her tongue as she took in the scene. Every one of her new shoes had been removed from their boxes, then placed in a raising pyramid shape on the floor. On the tip of the pyramid was the ugly broken figurine that the hot psychic had been so interested in. Shrieking with rage, she stormed the closet to put away her shoes. The ugly figurine was thrown carelessly over her shoulder. As she reached for the first shoe, an ice-cold hand wrapped around her wrist. Libby couldn't see the hand, only the indentation on her wrist where it was squeezing her. The cold from the invisible hand was radiating up her arm.

Shrieking with terror this time she ran from the closet not slowing until she reached the bedroom door. She risked a glance back over her shoulder. Standing at the foot of the bed was a smoky figure. It appeared to female with no distinguishable features. Libby could feel the anger coming off it in waves. With a whimper, she turned to flee from the house only to abruptly stop. Standing at the end of the hall was another smoky angry featureless figure. Sobbing with fear, she slid down the wall at the end of the hall, convinced she was going to die.

$$11$$

Chapter 11
"Men. Always carrying on about recipes. Why don't one of ya fetch me a beer and the paper?" I laid my southern accent on thick. The five men turned to look at me propped up against the cinderblock side of the concession hut my arms conveniently crossed under my boobs to emphasize them. "Then you can get back to your yakity yak."

Jesse rolled his eyes. "All you read is the comics. "

"I'm not going to read the news. That's just depressing." I countered with a knowing smile. His gaze hadn't strayed from the girls.

"And you don't drink beer." His eyes were saying suggestive things to mine now.

I pushed myself off the wall, with my hands on my hips. Playful disdain on my face I tugged on my husband's shirt. "So, fetch me the funnies and a Mountain Dew like a good little husband."

An OOO slipped out when I felt my phone vibrate in the inside pocket of my jacket. I gave a little extra jiggle as I pulled it out. Jesse's eyes followed the path of my hand.

I moved closer to Jess when I saw Michael's number on the screen. "Hello?"

The panicked tone of Michael coming across the phone had Jess jogging to get his truck and me hustling to find our child. Barefoot again, I ran across the grass. Most of the parents had migrated to the parking lot which lowered the chances of me getting cornered, but I didn't want to risk sinking a heel into the dirt and face planting.

I followed the sound of giggling to where the bleachers fence opened up to the field. Sure enough there was a group of teenage girls hanging on every word a group of footballers dropped. I was saddened to see my daughter's blonde head among the groupies. Jock boy was clearly enjoying they attention of all the girls surrounding him. Some one really needed to teach these girls some self-respect. It's not like he was the quarterback.

"Vanna!" She looked at me with irritation clearly on her face. "Gotta go. Now!"

I turned around to backtrack to the parking lot. I heard her saying her goodbyes. The fact that I was jogging seemed to clue her in that something was a foot. "What's up mom?"

"Tell you in the car." I huffed over my shoulder. My lungs were not used to this much exertion.

A few moments later, we hit the parking lot. My Jeep was actually fairly close since I wasn't technically in a parking spot. We hopped in the car and with a thump and some jiggling, we were on our way. I left some rubber on the pavement on the way out of the parking lot.

"Michael just called. The ghosts have become physical and aggressive. They attacked Libby." I explained to my daughter as I floored the Jeep to pass her father on the highway. Savannah waved at him as I flew around him. He might have more horsepower, but he didn't have my lead foot nor my need for speed.

I pulled into the drive with Jesse's Ram right on my tail a few moments later. The three of us scrambled out of the vehicles. My husband shot me a dirty look as we jogged towards Michael and Libby standing out by the curb. Libby, who was so pale she could be a ghost, was curling into herself while cradling her right wrist. Michael had his arms around her.

Jesse and Savannah's eyes were locked on that right wrist. To me it looked perfectly normal. Since looking at it wouldn't tell me anything of interest. I turned to glance at the house. In the window of the gym bedroom were two figures. Without consulting the psychics, I started for the house.

"What the hell did you two do?" I demanded. For a second, I could have sworn I saw remorse on their faces before they shimmered away. These two didn't strike me as evil or aggressive. Noticing that I had reached the porch without being stopped, I glanced backwards. My husband was actually about two feet behind me. "You getting anything?"

"Anger. Rage. Love. "His brow was furrowed in confusion. He reached around me to open the front door. Silently we walked down the hall to the master bedroom. I paused at the end of the hallway to look back at Jesse with a raised eyebrow. I could feel the energy here. Couldn't quite make out what kind of energy, but it was strong if I could feel it. "Anger. Think you trying to load a program on your old laptop."

I looked at him in horror. "I don't know what you mean by that."

He snorted. "You have apparently forgotten the reason you have a new laptop is because you got so mad trying to load Zoom on your old one, you threw it across the room. Barely missed my big screen TV."

"I told you, it slipped!" Disdainly, I threw my head back before walking into the master with all the dignity I could muster. I didn't really remember how the laptop became airborne. One moment I was beating on the keyboard, the next its innards were ricocheting around the living room. I stuck my head in the closet. Expensive shoes perfectly stacked and the creepy figurine was sitting like the star on top. "Huh."

"Rage is wrapped around the figurine. Reminds me of you on 635 when lanes are shut down." Jesse slid past me to circle the shoe tree. A shudder slid down my back. That was some serious rage. I'd been known to punch things in my car and swear more than Samuel L Jackson when I got stuck in that kind of traffic. Jesse and I walked the rest of the house. The energy was the strongest where Libby had been attacked. In the gym Jesse noticed some subtle energy that was apologetic or remorseful. The energy was too faint to be sure.

We were heading to the front door when a zing went down my back. There was a ghost in the house. A glance over my shoulder revealed Jesse was looking towards the kitchen. I clickity clacked across the living room as fast as my heels would allow. As I turned the corner into the kitchen, I saw the two ghosts whispering to each other in the kitchen. Obviously, I startled them judging by their surprised expressions. For a second, we just stared at each other.

I could finally see some details on them. Aqua bathrobe had short spiky white hair with makeup on one side of her face only, cute house shoes the same color as her robe, and a white H monogramed on the robe Seventies chick looked about the same as I remembered. Before I could find any further details, they dove out the wall.

I pulled my phone out to text Savannah to bring the occupants back in the house. Fairly sure they weren't going to return now that we were here.

The five of us settled around the kitchen table. All of us waved away Libby's offer of wine. Savannah needed a hard look before she declined. Libby shrugged then poured wine into a glass that was so huge I was fairly sure it was supposed to have tea lights or marbles in it. She settled into a chair by the bar with the bottle in front of her.

Libby recalled everything that happened after she got home from shopping. It was a truly terrifying story. But something felt off. The women that I kept seeing didn't seem violent. Jesse wasn't sensing anything melovant.

"May I?" Jesse pointed at Libby's wrist. She extended her right wrist to him after switching her glass to her left hand. He wrapped his hand around her wrist. It was so small his large hand swallowed it. "Babe?"

He beckoned me with a finger. I looked at it suspiciously. "Give me your hand." I patiently let him arrange my left hand around her wrist. "So, we are looking for a left-handed female that hates you. Any ideas?"

Something flashed in Libby's eyes before she shook her head and took a deep drink of her wine. Jess and I exchanged knowing glances. We had run into this before. Some people just refuse to be honest. Not wanting to press her just yet, we asked Michael what he had found out about the figurines.

An aunt remembered that the figurines had been bought new at the store. Another eye exchange between me and the hubby. Savannah spoke up before we could. "Doesn't that mean the attachment to the figurines happened after they were bought?"

Jess beamed with pride. "Yes. Most likely later in life. Were they important to anyone besides your late wife?"

Michael took a moment to look at the small picture on the wall. I hadn't noticed it. Inside the little circle frame was an attractive brunette with what looked like a wedding veil over mile high bangs. Interesting. During the initial walk through I had looked at pictures. I hadn't noticed her in any others. From the way Michael looked at it, I'd say that was Norma Rae. "Mary, I suppose."

"Do you have any pictures of Mary?" I asked Michael. He nodded. With a sad sigh he got up from his seat. A moment later he returned from the storage room at the end of the kitchen with one of those old flip books of pictures. Libby stared at the wall drinking wine while the guys turned the knob to flip through the pictures. I picked up the small telescope thingy and looked into it. There was seventies chick on a much better day. I handed it to Michael.

"Is this Mary?" Michael held it up to his eye. With a fond chuckle he shook his head.

"That is Ruby. Norma's sister." There was a twinkle in his eyes. With a smile he continued. "She died a year after Norma. "

"Any idea why she was in a gold lame jogging suit that screamed nineteen seventy something?

"She had an aneurism on Halloween. She was Blanche from The Golden Girls. When she fell, she landed in the punch bowl." A nod of understanding. "That's why her hair was red instead of the platinum blonde she's been most of her life."

"Any idea why she is haunting you and scaring your fiancé?" Time to get to the bottom of this mystery.

Michael shook his head in bewilderment. "We were always friends. Occasional co-conspirators. She

helped me throw a surprise birthday party once. Even made sure I got Norma exactly what she wanted

for gifts."

We flipped through the rest of the pictures looking for aqua robe woman. Sadly, she wasn't in there or

had age too much to be recognized. We threw in the towel a little before midnight. After goodbyes

were said, we climbed into our cars to drive home on autopilot.

When I pulled into our drive, I noticed Luna lying in the front yard, on the edge of the circle of light

produced by the porch light. Savannah helped Jesse carry our stuff into the house while I went to deal

with the cat. As I slowly approached her, she came towards me, rubbed my leg, and then went back to the shadows.

"Hey Luna." Sugar dripped from my tone. She was skittish and had to be sweet talked. Again, she rubbed

and ran. "What are you doing?"

Tired of the game she was playing, I scooped her up. Small little gray paws pushed against me as I

climbed the stairs to the front door where Savannah was waiting for us. I told my daughter good night

and carried the squirming cat to my room. We'd had her three years and she still resisted being handled.

When I dropped her onto the bed, Puck jumped up, sniffing all of her nooks and crannies. Luna hissed

and swatted him.

"Puck, out!" I pointed at the door. It was too late to deal with the animals. Puck of course, ignored me.

"GITOUTTAHERE!" Jesse didn't even bother sitting up as he ordered Puck out. Annoyingly, the dog

followed his command without question. I stuck my tongue out at him then went to the bathroom to get

ready for bed.

Shortly thereafter, I was crawling into bed. Luna crawled up on my pillow. "Uh no. That is mine." I slid

her over. "What is wrong with you tonight?"

"Sleeping here" My husband muttered sleepily. Luna demanded some love since I had moved her. I fell

asleep with Luna on my chest purring while I stroked her fur.

Feeling as if I had just gotten to sleep, I was awakened by claws kneading into my arm. "Ouch!"

I swatted the gray blur away. She rubbed her face on my mine. "What are you doing? You know better than to wake us up." Blurry eyed I looked over at my husband to see if she had woken him up too. He

was blissfully sleeping slacked jaw. Luna started kneading me again. "Why are you claws kitten sharp?"

I rolled over and scratched her head. She rolled her head into my hand and looked at me. Her eyes

seemed wrong, but I wasn't sure why. I drifted off wondering if she had lost weight.

12

Chapter 12

I was awoken the next morning by needles digging into my thighs. Somehow, I managed to squint an eye open to see Luna chewing on my leg. What the hell? Gently I pushed her away while attempting to scold her. Sadly, the only sounds coming out of me belonged on a nature soundtrack. Carefully I staggered into the bathroom to begin my day. Luna followed me. That was strange. She wasn't normally this needy.

She continued to follow me as I went about my morning routine. Jesse thankfully was already up so the coffee was already brewing. I padded barefoot to the closet after a scorching hot shower. Luna trailed behind me, batting at the belt to my robe.

"What is wrong with you?" Luna and I engaged in a tug of war for the belt while I opened the door. She dropped the belt with a hiss, bowing up into the classic spooked cat shape. Whipping my head around to the closet, I saw what had her fur up. A shriek escaped me when Jesse suddenly grabbed my arm to yank me behind him. The aqua bathrobe ghost was standing in the closet. I leaned around my burly husband to address her. "Hello. Whatcha doing in my closet?"

H gave my husband a dismissive look then focused her faded blue eyes on me. She wiggled a finger that appeared to have the beginning of arthritis on the knuckle at me. "Find someone else to help." Message delivered; she walked through the wall.

"Well, that was dramatic." Pushing Jesse out of the way I went into the closet, Luna attempting to climb my robe by the belt with every step. We both laughed when I let the robe drop on top of her. A naughty gleam came into Jesse's eyes as he took in me in my birthday suit. I let him kiss my neck for a moment before I pushed him away as his hand started to wander down to my southern regions. "Breakfast isn't going to fix itself you know."

"I know what my breakfast is going to be." We giggled while closing the closet the door.

Jesse had me pushed up against the door kissing his way down my neck, clearly planning on having some adult fun when he lifted his head with a disgusted sigh. He looked towards the wall to the bathroom with squinted eyes. With a tug, he pulled me away from the door. His stride stiff, he walked out of the closet. I shrugged into my robe on the way to the bathroom. "Oh my" I whispered when I walked in.

Heed my Warning was written across my mirror in the steam left over from my shower. *Dire consequences* was written in the steam on Jesse's mirror.

Oh no she did not! I had just cleaned those mirrors. Obviously, Jesse agreed since his teeth were clenched while his green eyes glared at the mirrors.

"Oh, hell to the no! Come in my house and not just threaten me, interrupt morning fun time but, write on my mirrors? Oh, this ends now!" The unicorn slippers on my feet muffled the stomping on the hardwood floors as I hurried to the closet. Muttering about ghosts daring to invade my privacy, especially while my husband was feeling dirty, I yanked a shirt off a hanger. After I shoved my arms through the sleeves of a Kansas City Chiefs shirt celebrating Mahomes, I shimmied into my favorite low-rise jeans with excessive bling on the butt. Jesse watched with an amused look as I pulled my cowboy boots down off the top shelf of the closet. I stuck my tongue out at him as I pulled a pair of long socks out of his drawer.

Jesse leaned up against the door frame to the closet while I sat on the bed to shove my feet into boots I only wore for ass kicking or hanging in the country with my in-laws. They always make me feel unstoppable. Probably why I needed them when I dealt with my mother-in-law. The woman hated me. She claimed I was too city for her taste and somehow managed to bespell her son into moving into town with me. Truth was my banana bread was scarfed down faster than hers every thanksgiving. She hadn't even bothered to make hers for several years now. If these boots could keep me grounded while dealing with that shrew, they could undoubtedly handle two ghosts that were looking to cause trouble.

"What if aqua robe is Libby's ex-Mother-in-Law? That could explain the hostilities." Luna trailed behind me crying as she tried to figure eight between my feet. "Did you feed the cats this morning?"

"MMM" My husband responded from the kitchen where he was plating biscuits and gravy.

"No time for breakfast. I got my ass kicking boots on!" I walked around the bar to the counter where there was a huge mug with steam coming out of it. A sigh of contentment slipped out with the first taste of the coffee. He could make my coffee better than any barista out there. A wicked gleam entered his eyes as he watched me sip the coffee he had made for me.

"I know how you can tip me."

I shot him a lascivious look over the rim of my mug. "You wanna go exorcise some ghosts and then get naked? Maybe in the truck along some back road?" I wiggled my eyebrows. Not that he noticed. His eyes watched the way I made the girls wiggle too. His eyes rose to mine as he drug me over to him by a belt loop.

"EWWWWW! NO! You need Jesus!" Savannah came out of the hallway. She deliberately walked between us to push us apart. Her long blonde hair was pulled into a ponytail, the end swaying between her shoulder blades. She was still in her dancing coffee cup PJs. Only her glasses were on her face. It was so rare to see her without makeup or lashes or her contacts. I loved the few times a week I got to see my daughter. She was as beautiful as her father was handsome. Sometimes I had to wonder if there was any of me in there. After she separated us, her eyes fell on the table. "Oh. Biscuits and gravy! Thanks dad!"

"Breakfast then ghost ass kicking." The three of us settled around the table for the breakfast the man of the house had so thoughtfully provided for us. The man could make gravy. Damn, I married well. I was washing my first bite down with a giant swig of coffee when Luna jumped up on the table to start licking my plate.

"Luna! What is wrong with you?" My words had no effect nor did me swatting her away. Unblinking brownish eyes stared at me almost daring me to shoo her again. "Does she seem different to you?"

The snickers from my family had me giving them dirty looks. "Wanna share the joke?"

Jesse got out of his chair to retrieve his phone from the bowl by the door. Odd. He had extremely strict feelings about phones at the table. He stood beside my chair for a minute before placing the phone in front of me with a picture of Luna open on it. Oh. Nonchalantly I scratched my head while looking away from my family. Still keeping my eyes from meeting theirs I clicked his phone off. Living with psychics wasn't all that it was cracked up to be. "When did you realize?"

Jesse chortled at me. "As soon as I saw her this morning."

"She looked off to me last night." Savannah shrugged a shoulder as took the daintiest bite of her breakfast.

"Who might you be?" I picked up the grey tabby that was chowing down on my bacon to look her in her brown eyes that should have been a more aqua marine. A glance at their undercarriage reveled that he was a neutered male. "Guess we should post him on the lost and found pages."

While Jesse got the new kitty settled on the floor with what was left of my breakfast, I made a new plate. On my way back to the table I threw a glance at the intruder. I felt a bit sleazy for sleeping with a cat I didn't know. Hopefully, Luna would forgive me.

"What makes you think she is the mother-in-law?" Jesse waited until I was settled at the table again to ask the question he should already know the answer to.

"Anger, rage, and love. That's what you said you felt from the ghosts. Isn't that about what you feel when your mother looks at me?" My words were a little muffled since I was talking and licking gravy off my thumb at the same time. Savannah scoffed at my words. Her dad gave me an amused look.

"Yeah no. Leave out love." I stuck my tongue out at her to be silly. As her mother I was both proud and worried that she had picked up on the undercurrents of the family dynamics. She swiped a piece of bacon off my plate in retaliation.

"She has developed a " Jesse paused, probably looking for the right word. One that wouldn't contradict what his daughter was sensing, yet, not hurting my feelings. Not that he really needed to worry about that. I didn't like that red neck heifer that was his mother any more than she liked me. "grudging respect for your mother."

"Warn me before you dump that big of a pile of bullshit." I gestured towards my boots. "I'm wearing my favorite boots."

"Oh, like that's the first time they have ever had shit on them." My daughter almost snorted gravy out her nose when she realized she had vocalized her thoughts instead of keeping them to herself. Not falling out of my chair laughing took real effort. Jesse just stared at his baby girl. A snort of laughter escaped my nose. Jesse's eyes rolled towards the basement door. Savannah slapped a hand over her mouth. "I think I was possessed."

"That's a dollar in the swear jar!" We all jumped as my grandmother came into the dining room. "See Holly Lee, this is why you need to be more careful about the example you set. Your husband made breakfast. You swear like a sailor. You allow pets on the table. How is she to become a proper lady and marry a man worthy of our family?"

"Isn't there a bingo hall for you to haunt?" My inquiry might have lost some of its bite since I was batting a cat tail out of my face. We were going to have to teach the furry little Don Juan table etiquette. Rule one was never ever give Grandma Eleanor any kind of ammunition.

"Hmmp." Eleanor's blue eyes lasered into mine for a moment. I looked away to get the new kitty off the table. Undoubtedly, she took that as a victory. "Call your mother. She is talking about turning all the fixtures rustic bronze! I just polished all the brass in that house a month before I crossed."

"Savannah, clear the table." I stood up with the kitty in my arms. Without another word I carried him around Grandma to go into the laundry room. Before we left, I had to make sure he knew where to do his business. Jesse went into the kitchen to put up the leftovers while Savannah did as I asked by clearing the table and rinsing the dishes.

After we had finished our tasks, we reconvened at the table. Thankfully, Grandma had left. I had an urge to call all the bingo halls to warn them of a potential spectral visitor. Jesse spoke first. "If she is the ex-mother-in-law, the ending had to be atrocious between Libby and her ex. "

"Maybe he didn't like how much she spent on shoes." Savannah piped up with. Both of us swung our heads towards her. "She was wearing red bottom shoes. Do you know how much those go for?"

I looked at Jesse and shrugged. He shrugged back. With a flare, I whipped my phone out of my back pocket. Savannah giggled at me before I even launched a search browser. "Something you wanna say?"

"They are Louboutin and sell for about eight hundred dollars." Savannah didn't even look up from playing with the new kitty.

"Eight hundred US dollars?" Jesse's eyes were close to bulging out of his face. My shoulders shook with mirth. He never understood the cost of beauty. Amusement was sparkling in our daughter's eyes as she nodded. Panic shimmered in his eyes when they locked on mine. "Do you have any of these Louie Boutin things?"

"If I had eight hundred dollars just lying around, we would have one of those reclining beds." I dismissed this ridiculous line of questioning with a wave of my hand. Hopefully he never looked into how much my collectibles cost. "Time to kick some ghost ass. Savannah, are you going with us?"

"UH yeah." She flew out of the chair so fast her long blonde hair whipped around to slap her in the face. I loaded the dishwasher while Jesse got his shoes put on.

"You really think you have this all figured out?" Answering his question was not my top priority since his mouth was nibbling on my ear.

"HMMMM." Was the best I could do. I started to lean back into his body. THWACK. My eyes flew open as a furry paw with claws slapped me in the face. What the hell? Don Juan was sitting on the counter. Once he saw I was looking at him, he started purring and rubbing on me. "I don't think he wants to share me."

Jesse was still glaring at the cat that had blocked him when Savannah came bopping down the hall in leggings and what amounted to a sports bra. Oh, she wasn't leaving the house like that. Before I could find the words, Jesse silently pointed towards her room. She gave him a belligerent look but returned to her room. A few moments later she came out with a men's unbuttoned shirt thrown over the bra.

"Best we got time for." I said as I ushered everyone out the garage door. My time was better served evicting unwelcomed ghosts instead of trying to get a teenager to cover her mid rift. The three of us climbed into Jesse's truck.

13

Chapter 13

Jesse pulled the truck to a smooth stop in front of the gray brick house. My boots made a thunking noise as I hopped down from the truck. For a moment I stood tall staring down my adversary, tapping my boot to a random beat in my head. These ghosts were going down. The front of the house seemed calm. The shiver running up and down my spine said otherwise. My boots continued thunking out a tempo that I decided was my war song while I stalked up the driveway. My stride was full of determination as I strutted to the front door. I was settling this issue today.

On the porch I raised my hand to knock on the thick wooden door. Libby swung the door open before I could knock. Quickly adjusting to the change, I lowered my arm as I charged through the door with my game face unwavering. My boots thunking on the cheap laminate flooring continued my war song until I stopped in the middle of the living room.

"All right! Show yourselves now!" The command echoed in the mostly empty room. Looking around, I realized all the knickknacks and wall décor was gone. Curiously, I turned to Libby. "Redecorating?"

Libby gave me a disbelieving look. Her brow furrowed above her flashing brown eyes. "I didn't know what else might have some ghastly attachment to it. I chucked everything out."

A glance around the room revealed my husband and child were missing. Odd. It wasn't like him to leave me unattended in a haunted house. Michael wasn't there either. "Did you notice where my posse went off to?"

She walked towards the back door beside the fireplace. Her eight-hundred-dollar shoes clicking all the way. "I wanted to throw all the possibly haunted junk in the trash. But Michael wanted to keep it." She rolled her eyes. "Michael is out there now. I saw your husband and daughter go to the side gate."

On the other side of the door was a beautiful screened in covered patio that ran the length of the house. At the center of the patio was a screen door that we went through. Obviously, Libby was a pro at wearing heels. She stayed on the stone path. My boots wouldn't sink into the ground like her stilettos would, which allowed me to walk beside her. We seemed to be heading for the small barn shaped shed in the back corner of the yard. It sat in the furthest point from the house with its two sides touching the six-foot privacy fence and appeared to have had recently been installed. The gray plastic sides showed no dirt that I could see. The double doors were open. My war song returned for a few beats when I stepped on to the small porch. There wasn't enough room for me to join the trio already inside, so I stopped when I was close enough to stick my head in the door.

Inside the shed Michael was vigilantly wrapping a beautiful blue bell that had probably been hand painted in bubble wrap. Once it was protected, he carefully placed it inside a huge tub with wheels that sat beside him. A Lego looking lid laid next to the tub. For a moment wondered how much the tub had cost. My Halloween/Fall décor had outgrown its current containment system. I gave an internal sigh; this wasn't the time. Beside him was my family. Savannah was pulling bric-a-brac out of trash bags. Jesse was meticulously wrapping framed pictures in blankets. Beside him was a shelving unit that other pictures had already been slid into. I wasn't a psychic like my family, but even I could feel the sadness sweeping though the small building. Libby settled herself on a camp chair on the deck. In the drink holder was a stemless wine glass. I assumed the pinkish liquid in it was wine.

"Who's the lady in the aqua robe? Name starts with H?" I used my mommy voice. One of these two people knew who she was. I knew it. Michael shook his head negative without looking up from the Beatles plate he was wrapping. Libby gave an indifferent shrug. An agitated sigh escaped me. I pointed a finger at each of them. "One of you know. She is connected to you. Spill."

With the Beatles plate secure, Michael looked up at me. "She could be a friend of Ruby's." He made a helpless hand gesture and shrugged. "I have no idea why they would haunt us like this." After giving himself a shake, he took a figurine from Savannah which he began wrapping.

"Aqua robe lady popped by our house this morning." Quickly I gave them a rundown of what had happened this morning. Minus the dirty parts involving my hubster. "I know the vibe I got off her. It's the same one I get from my MIL. She's one of your mother's, MIL, or an overly protective aunt."

"Your mother-in-law would break your TV with your designer shoe?" Libby's tone was close to sneering. I was really beginning to not like her. She had come off as a decent person every time I had met her. However, today she wasn't so likeable.

"Of course not. That would upset her precious baby boy and that isn't allowed. Nah, she has better ways of dealing with an interloper like me." I launched into a story that always won the who has the worst mother-in-law contests. During pregnancy I had gained almost sixty pounds. While Jesse and I were in the hospital waiting for

Savannah to make her big debut, my mother-in-law was at our house shopping in my closet. She helped herself to any of my clothes that she liked or thought her daughters might want. Shock would be a mild word to describe what I felt when she showed up at the hospital the next day in my favorite camisole and cardigan. When I confronted her, she justified her actions by saying there was no chance I would lose enough weight to wear the clothes again and should be grateful that she had removed the clothes from the house so I wouldn't feel bad about my "mom bod." She still denied it to this day but I always felt she did it to punish me for not letting her be in the delivery room. Fury had seeped into my tone by the end of my story.

"I did get all your clothes back." Jesse injected from his picture wrapping station. A petulant look sent his direction had him chuckling. "Ok, I also changed the locks with coded ones."

"She stole your clothes?" Libby was giving me a once over that made it clear she wasn't impressed with my style. At least I was in real clothes. She was again in her active wear pants. Her shirt didn't even cover her ass. Everyone knows if you wear those kinds of pants your shirt should cover your ass! Learned that in middle school when stirrup pants came back in style.

"Yep. So, who hates you enough to destroy your stuff and keep you on edge?" My question was directed at Libby. I was certain aqua robe was her ghost, not Michael's. Once we figured out who she was, then we could figure out why they had teamed up.

"No one." Her tone was firm. If I couldn't see her eyes, I might have fallen for it. I'd been doing this a long time. Lies live in the eyes, no matter how well hidden, they were still there. My gut said she was the villain of this piece. A glance at Jesse confirmed it.

"Mrs. H! Please show yourself." I commanded the sky. Hopefully, she was not only listening but wanted to tell her story. We all looked around. Nothing happened. Hooking a thumb towards the house I addressed my husband. "I'm going ghost hunting."

"They are both here. Keep an eye out. Their anger is filling the house." Jesse's voice echoed slightly in the rolling tote beside Michael. He stood up holding the non-broken figurine of the girl on the phone. "Take this with you."

"It's glowing like the sun." Savannah squinted her eyes as she looked at it. I looked at the creepy faced figurine in my hand. If it had an aura I couldn't see it. But I'd learned when a psychic told you take something, you should do just that, so I waved it at them before turning to step off the porch of the shed.

"Ok." My boots began playing my song again as I took the stone path back to the house. After a moment I heard Libby's heels clicking behind me. Briefly I wondered if the clicking was her war song. I ignored her questions of where I was going. Quickly we reached the screen door to the patio. I held it open for Libby. She huffed at me as she passed. At the door into the house, she didn't return the favor. Oh yeah. I had found my villain.

Once inside, I headed straight for the kitchen. I figured it was the most changed room in the house. Change is a terrific way to piss off the ghosts. Boots singing my song, I strutted to the sink to place the figurine in the window over it. "Ruby? Mrs. H?"

Clapping caught my attention. I swung my head to the dining area. Sitting in one of the chairs was Ruby. Now that I knew it was a costume, I paid more attention to her face than her clothes. Intelligence mixed with amusement in her brown eyes, her hair was cut into what was I'm sure a cute short cut had it not been trapped forever having been doused in punch and sticking up weirdly. I had to wonder if the sky-high heels on her feet had played any part in her falling into the punch bowl. That was one of the tragedies for ghosts. They were forever trapped how they looked at the moment of death.

Thankfully, their faces didn't get locked or that would be traumatizing to those of us that could see them.

"Figure it out yet, kid?"

14

Chapter 14

I finally got the damn butternut squash peeled and chopped. Dumping the pieces into the baking dish was incredibly satisfying. I threw the pan into the oven before I wrapped Band-Aids around the fingers I had sliced up peeling the damned squash. Satisfied I wouldn't bleed on anything, I continued dinner. My mental fingers were crossed that Grandma Eleanor would stay away. While I dipped chicken in eggs and breadcrumbs, I thought back to the morning.

Ruby was sitting at the kitchen table taunting me. She was a feisty one. Her accent was not southern. There was undoubtedly Northern hostility in her tone.

"Where you from Ruby?" I didn't really care. I just needed to delay her answers until the rest of the living could get in here. She shot me a look that clearly questioned my intelligence.

"Ohio. Moved up there right outta high school with my husband. Had to lose the drawl. " I nodded. The kitchen suddenly felt crowded as my family and Michael joined us. The psychics were looking at Ruby while Michael was looking at me like I was a squirrelly acting dog. Libby was perched on a bar stole drinking her pink wine.

"Ok Ohio, why don't we see if we can break this down." I pointed at the figurine on the windowsill. "You showed up I bet when the other figurine got broken."

Ruby gave a nod. Michael was falling my eyeline to his deceased sister-in-law. His jaw dropped when I said Ohio. Ruby was looking at him. Her fondness for him shimmering in her eyes.

"I've popped in from time to time over the years to make sure he's ok. Seems I had been negligent in checking on him. This hussy snuck in." Savannah and I followed her squinted eyes to Libby at the bar. "There I was soaking up the sun on a cruise ship in the middle of the Atlantic when I felt something odd. Popped in here to check on him. Found him in bed with the strumpet. Ask him what he sees in such a flashy girl! Never his kind of gal."

"What's that red head phantom saying about me?' Libby's words were slightly slurred. Glazed brown eyes tried to focus on the chair that I was talking to. "I didn't break that creepy faced piece of clutter!"

"Less creepy than your face!' Ruby was standing beside the tipsy woman of the house now. Libby grasped her chest with a sharp inhale. At a guess I'd say she felt the ice-cold finger Ruby was poking on her chest. Eerie laughter filtered in from the closet at the end of the kitchen. Aqua robe strolled through the wall.

"Jigs really up wouldn't you say Ruby?" Aqua robe was definitely Southern. Not Texan. More like North Carolina. She walked through the bar to look Libby in the eye. "Strumpet is too kind of a word for this one."

Jesse cleared his throat. I glanced his way reluctantly. There was about to be drama and I didn't want to miss it. He had a raised eyebrow. I waved an absent hand his way. "Savannah be a dear and translate for the ghost deaf. OK Mrs. H. What should we call ya? Aqua just seems wrong."

She reached a smooth looking alabaster hand out to me. "Harper Wellington. Of the North Carolina Wellingtons. Please forgive the casual attire. I had the misfortune of passing while preforming my nightly ritual."

I took her hand as best I could since we couldn't really touch. It was freezing with a slight charge to it. This close I could see the fire still burning in her eyes. I'd bet my Funko pop collection this woman had ruled her roost with an iron hand and a sharp mind. Dropping my hand, she turned to Libby with a bitter expression twisting her face. "This harlot knows what she did to deserve this. Ask her about Gregory."

"Who's Gregory?" Since I was looking her in the eye I saw Libby flinch when I said the name. She shrugged a delicate shoulder while downing what was left of her pink wine. "So, you don't know the name Gregory Wellington?"

Michael was watching Libby close. I couldn't remember how long they had been together, but I bet it was long enough for him to know her tells. Without a word he went into the closet at the end of the kitchen Harper had come out of. My family and his watched him. From the corner of my eye, I saw Libby pour more pink wine. Harper had moved to the bay window that faced the backyard. Michael came back carrying a metal flask. Still in complete silence he filled a glass with ice. Then he went and stood in front of Libby. Maintaining eye contact, he poured the contents of the flask over ice. He swirled it around then took a long drink.

"Michael!" Libby's voice was sharp, riddled with censure. "You promised to stop drinking whiskey. You know I can't stand the smell of it!"

" Liberty Walker, who is Gregory Wellington?" There was fierceness in Michael's tone that surprised me. He had struck me as a very bland easy-going person. Perhaps there was a backbone in there that I hadn't noticed. A glance at Jesse revealed he wasn't surprised, so I had to guess he had a fairly strong aura. She swirled her wine and refused to look at him. Michael poured another drink while we waited.

A whiny sigh that rivaled anything that had ever come out of Savannah emerged from Libby. "Fine, Greg was my fiancé. Things went bad and our relationship ended. Just like this one." Libby glared at her apparent ex-fiancé with glazed eyes for a moment then stormed off to the master. We all jumped a little when the door slammed.

I looked at Mrs. Wellington. "Alright Mrs. W. It's up to you to fill in the blanks."

"I wish my Gregory had found a girl like you. His father would have been entranced by your spirit. He would have called malarkey on you seeing ghosts, but he would have overlooked it. " Gardenia wafted off the opaque white hand that fluttered by my face. "Gregory didn't take my death well. He went a bit wayward. Began hanging out in low rent districts. They had dollar Jello shots!" The disdain was clear in her voice. "That attracted the most common kind of girls."

On one of his trips to the wrong side of town, he had met Libby Walker. At the time she was a big, boobed platinum blonde in low cut halter tops that bared her mid drift paired with hot pants that trolled the bars looking for men with money to sink her hooks into. Gregory was angry that his mother had died. Harper had taken to haunting her son, hoping he would feel her presence and return to the right side of the tracks. Instead, he fell for the old oops I spilled my drink on you routine. In no time, she was moved into his penthouse apartment enjoying everything his money could buy.

Finally, he gave into family pressure to introduce her to them. He took his now fiancé to the family home. One glance at the social climber and his father knew exactly what kind of girl she was. He suggested Gregory have his fun with the harlot but, he was forbidden to marry her. His father held the purse strings in the family. If Gregory defied him, he would be cut off.

Unfortunately, Gregory was a stubborn boy in his mid-twenties. There was no reasoning with him. He gave Libby Harper's engagement ring. His father was so incensed he cut off Gregory and demanded the ring be returned. Gregory refused. His father threw them out of the penthouse while seizing all their belongings. Within a month Gregory was in rehab for a drinking problem after totaling his late model sports car. Libby had skipped town, with the ring plus a few thousand in cash she had managed to sneak out of the safe. She sold the ring to a jeweler. She had been staying at the Four Seasons in Las Colinas for a brief time when she met Michael on the golf course.

Being an experienced hustler, Libby was engaged and living with Michael in short order. Harper had been unsuccessfully haunting her the whole time. She had not yet learned how to move objects or make noises. Libby bought a few things to upgrade Michael's house using the money stolen from Gregory. Thanks to an overheard conversation with a friend, Harper learned Libby planned to upgrade the house and then make Michael sell it when his money ran out. She would demand her fair share of the equity since she had contributed to the house. Libby figured it wouldn't be much longer. The Rover and her credit cards were draining his retirement fund quickly. Harper was enraged enough to finally move something. The creepy faced figurine. That action is what attracted Ruby.

Harper and Ruby teamed up to try and protect Michael from Libby. Since Ruby had been a ghost for decades, she knew how to haunt properly. Rage that another good man was going to be destroyed made Harper a fast learner. The shoe to the TV was her first thrown object.

Savannah finishing the translation of the story for the ghost impaired paired perfectly with Libby stomping out of the bedroom with her bags. She gave us a disgusted look then started for the door. I stepped in front of her. "Who did you sell the ring to?"

"Why should I tell you?" She managed to sneer and slur at the same time.

"Because if you don't, I'm going to send a ghost army to haunt your every move. I do know how to summon demons too. It's not easy to get rid of one those if they are directed to you." I contorted my face into a fake sympathy look. There was no chance of the demons, but she didn't know that. "Or worse I will send my mother-in-law to your place."

She spit out the name of jeweler. She darted around me to the hook hanging by the door.

"Where are my keys?"

Jesse held them up from the couch he was leaning against. "You are drunk off your ass. I called you a ride. It'll be out front in a minute. You should wait outside." He picked up her bags like a gentleman. Then he tossed them out into the yard like a baggage handler. Libby shrieked and chased after them. Jesse closed and locked the door. We went back to the kitchen arm in arm.

Michael was sitting at the table drinking whiskey from a bottle he had unearthed from somewhere. His gaze was fixed on the chair Ruby had been sitting. Ruby was making the lazy Susan on the table spin very slowly while chatting away. Savannah was happily being go between helping the two reconnect. Michael looked at the table. "Have you seen Norma?"

Ruby walked around the table to cover his hand with hers. "Norma popped in from time to time. She was thrilled when you moved on. She didn't want you to be alone."

Ruby promised to get Norma to pop in again. We promised to get word to Harper's family about where the ring was. Before we made our goodbyes, Jesse slid Michael the engagement ring he had slipped off Libby's finger. "She didn't need this anymore."

After hugs and a few tears, the three of us climbed into Jesse's truck. He dropped us girls at the house then ran to the store for me. His eyebrows almost reached his hairline when he read the list I gave him.

The garage door went up as I put the chicken into bake. Jesse walked into the house, dropping his keys in the bowl. With a quick glance at me, he opened the bags he carried on the table. "Any idea why Paul is asking if I can fashion Uno cards into roses?"

Shaking my head, I walked out of the pantry with a package of cookies that I placed next to the milk on the bar. My husband had laid everything out in a line on the table like it was evidence. "Is there an infestation I need to know about?" He raised an eyebrow. "Or are we going to war?"

I walked beside two boxes of sage smudge sticks, five pounds of sea salt, and two gallons of holy water to hand him a cookie. "War sounds right."

Leaning in, I stole a quick kiss and shoved his cookie in my mouth before he could protest. He shot me a flirty how dare you look when he passed me on his way to get another cookie. Gentleman that he is, he brought me a mug of milk on his way back. Silently he stared at me as I swished the milk around my mouth to get rid of the cookie crumbs. "War?"

"The Swallow House is for sale." Frozen with the cookie halfway in his mouth he gazed unfocused at me. Then Jesse gave a hard blink and shook his head to reset himself. He chugged his milk after finishing the cookie. His eyes locked on me.

"I thought the trustees agreed not to sell." I made a helpless whatcha going to do motion with my hands. My eyes slid a longing look at the cookies on the bar. Jesse let out a silent chuckle. Proving I was right to marry the man, he grabbed the pack of cookies along with a beer and milk carton. We settled at the table. Our coping mechanisms on display, me dunking cookies in milk and him drinking his beer. "Are they disclosing that the house has multiple demon portals in it?"

"No clue. They didn't tell me. It popped up on one of my socials." I scarfed down another cookie. "I should also mention that yesterday mom ripped out the hallway-built ins."

"Oh, dear God no!" My husband's face loss color and looked slightly clammy. He seemed to understand the significance. "Do we have enough salt to surround the whole house?

E pilogue
The alarms had me cracking an eye open. No signs of ghosts. Always a good start to the day. I hated waking up to the sight of a guy that went through a windshield. Or worse my grandmother in her orange puffy vest. No good day ever started that way. Last night my BFF Violet had texted about two houses she wanted me to check for spooky activity. She wanted to exploit my ability to see and hear the dead. No one told me growing up that part of being a ghost translator meant giving up sleep. As I laid there trying to convince myself to get up, I could hear cartoons playing in the living room. My early bird husband had probably already had a full day since he got up as soon as the sun peeked over the horizon. I rolled out of bed at the ungodly hour of nine am on a Sunday. There were days I wondered why I had married a morning person. At least he wasn't singing this morning. I hated waking up to him singing happy songs. *Wake Me Up Before You Go Go* was one of his favorites. He was lucky he was cute.

Groggy, I threw on some jeans and a black tee shirt with a little mummy gnome on it. A quick trip to the bathroom to do my hair and put on my fall latte earrings before slipping a pair of black sandals on my feet. Still not fully awake, I wandered out to the kitchen where my family awaited me. My loving husband was at the stove scooping up some kind of pancake wrap thingy that smelled like it had sausage and eggs in it. Oh right, this was why I married him. He of course was already dressed for the day in a flannel shirt and jeans. He stilled smelled of his bath gel, yet his dark blonde hair and goatee were both dry. He'd left some stubble on his jaw line. Briefly I wondered if the sun was even shining when he showered. Our teen daughter Savannah was sitting at the table, still in her dancing kitty pjs, nibbling on a small pancake with a side of eggs. Her long blonde hair was pulled up in bun on the top of her head. It was refreshing to see her bare face. Girls today wore fake lashes constantly it seemed. Her green eyes didn't need any enhancements in my opinion.

"Are you sure you don't need me to go with you?" My husband Jesse asked as he handed me my pancake wrap in a paper towel.

"So far there's been no soul of any kind. I'll call if I need you." He looked relieved. I knew he would have come but also knew he had a poker game scheduled for later in the day. Thankfully the child had plans to go to the outlet mall with friends which kept her from begging to join me. I loved my offspring but Vi and I needed to discuss what kind of debauchery she had gotten up to lately. Ever since her husband ran off to California, she was working her way through the most eligible bachelors and other hotties she found along the way. "We can pretend you saved me from the evil demon later. Heads up. Your reward will be dirty."

A devilish smile spread across Jesse's face. Then he planted a kiss that left me breathless on me. Our child ewwed. I giggled out a good-bye on my way to the garage.

Twenty minutes later I pulled my purple Jeep up to a white stucco monstrosity of a house in Flower Mound my GPS led me to. Multiple cars were already parked along the street. A huge sign proclaimed an open house today. There were a couple of cars that I didn't recognize the emblem on. Guess I wasn't ready to run with Vi's crowd.

If memory served, the neighborhood now sat where a horse farm used to be. Despite my vows to never grow old, I was now to the point of saying I remember when this was nothing but fields and trees. Sighing, I looked at what might be my BFF's new home. The lantern sconces were bigger than the tires on my car. The front was just a huge wall of white stucco and black trim. Little awnings over the windows made it slightly interesting but ultimately soulless. As I stood there I realized that every fourth house had the same facade, I shuttered. This had to be one of the creepiest neighborhoods I'd ever been in. Master planned cookie cutter homes. Creepy. I opened my inner eye to see if there were any souls on the inside. Sighing I leaned against my Jeep drinking my golden eagle frozen coffee from Dutch Bros.

Momentarily Vi came out of the eight-foot double front doors. Sashaying down the walkway that gleamed like it had some kind of product mixed into the concrete to make it look like granite (given the neighborhood, it might actually be some kind of fancy shiny stone.), she was the picture of grace. Long honey blonde hair flowed down her shoulders covering part of her gauzy orange sleeve-less shirt. Black shorts and Halloween themed slip ons encased her feet. Once she got close enough, I saw she had little black cats with witch hats earrings on with a matching necklace.

"What do you mean you aren't coming in?" She waved her phone at me that also had a Halloween case on it.

"Oh good. You got my text." I was still leaning against my Jeep. Receiving the kind of annoyed look only a loved one can give you, I decided to expand on my comments. "There's a clinger in there."

Vi looked back over her shoulder with concern. A clinger was a lonely ghost that liked to chat and didn't believe in alone time. A Velcro ghost if you will. If I went in there and they realized I could see them, it could take me weeks to shake them off. She joined me in leaning against the car after I handed her the fancy lemonade I had picked up for her.

"This one was gorgeous on the inside. Could you just exorcise it?"

"Not a good idea. That might invite other things in. Best to buy in a different neighborhood." Looking wistful, she nodded before dusting her backside off from any dirt my Jeep might have had on it. Slipping her designer sunglasses on, she headed for her Aston Martin parked on the curb in front of me, calling for me to follow her.

Stepping out of my Jeep I looked at the huge mariner blue modern farmhouse I had followed Vi to. It had cape cod style siding with bright white accents. The columns that lined the front porch were ornate as was the railing that enclosed the porch. Obviously, a new build since the trees were barely more than saplings, the grid lines of the sod were still very visible. A quick psychic look around revealed nothing of interest. If ghosts hung out in these parts, I couldn't feel them. While I was doing a psychic look, VI went ahead on it to the house. Once I made it up the long walk, the front door had been left open.

"Hello?" I called as I walked through the marble floored foyer. The walls were lined with bright white wainscoting while the walls were white as well. Vi's voice came from the left. Following it took me though a formal sitting area that had dark hardwood flooring and more white on white. A few chairs had been placed to show potential placement. Finding a hallway, I wandered around to the back of the house where VI was in the spacious kitchen. White shaker cabinets lined the wall. Marble tile was on the floor and back splash. In the middle of the room an island took up most of the floor space. Vi was on the floor looking at the storage space available in the island. As I walked to her, I noticed the counter tops were also marble.

"What do you think?" Her tone didn't indicate which way she was leaning. I decided to stay neutral.

"I think it's a blank slate. Very neutral." My tongue clicked a few times as I looked around. Curious, I opened a door on the far side. Found the pantry. Definitely huge. Not surprising since the house was five thousand square feet. "A lot you could do with it."

Vi looked at me before sticking her head in the pantry. "Hmmm. Not enough room for a big deep freezer. I'll have to check if the laundry room has space for one. How did it go with ghost hunting yesterday?"

Wandering around the house trying to locate the laundry room I filled her in on my Saturday. She snickered when I made the comparison between my mother-in-law and the ghost. "Another reason to be thankful for my divorce. No more mother-in-law. At least yours never sent Jesse links to Reddit posts about abusive wives and offering to help him escape your clutches."

"No, mine just tried to setup my fiancé at a town fair." I scoffed. Finally, we found the laundry room. It was on the back side of the house at the end of a hall that had the downstairs master and den off it.

"I remember that." Vi's giggle echoed off the white marble tiled walls. "Isn't that when you scarred that poor girl?"

Shrugging I refused to answer while snickering. Soon after Jesse and I had gotten engaged his little hometown had its annual chili cook off. While I had stopped off at the ladies' room my lovey mother-in-law to be was introducing my newly minted fiancé to the cute new girl. She had met the girl in line at the grocery store shortly after she had moved to town. When I joined the group, the cute little brunette was batting her eyes at Jesse. Quickly I introduced myself to the girl wearing a Depeche Mode concert tee. Interestingly he was Jesse's favorite band at the time.

"Oh! Gloria mentioned you. You're his sister, right?" The girl was cute. Her brown hair spilled past her shoulders in a riot of curls. Hazel eyes glinted with interest when they flicked back to my man. Clearly Gloria wanted to play dirty. Challenge accepted.

"Sweet of her to mention me." I planted a kiss on Jesse that should have been x rated. I heard the new chick gasp. I turned to look at her beside Gloria. "What? Family gets first dibs right?"

"Not nice mom." Jesse admonished his mother. He lifted my left hand to his mother's preferred girl. "Holly is my fiancé. We are not related."

"But will be soon. I know how excited Gloria is to be my new mommy." Death glares shot from my eyes as Jesse drug me off to find a funnel cake.

Vi shook her head as I finished my story. "Was that also when you barked at her the whole trip?"

Snorting, I opened the door in the master bedroom that led to a private patio area. "On the drive home after the fair she accused me of acting like a bitch in heat. So, I only barked at her for the rest of our visit. Still do on occasion just to piss her off."

As we finished the tour of the house I inquired about her evening with Paul. They were still dancing when Jesse and I left the bar.

An impish look that made her hazel eyes gleam responded to my question. Just shy of giving too much information she filled me in on our depraved night with the tall, dark, handsome, and apparently inventive playboy. They had gone back to his place in Copell. They had a few glasses of wine. Danced to some Marvin Gaye. A few more drinks. Then played strip uno. Instead of drawing cards, they lost clothing. I stopped her when she got to the part where she was in her undies and he only in his watch.

Her story concluded as we finished the tour for the ground floor. The house had a fancy staircase that the bottom step was about six feet wide, and they narrowed for the next few steps until they became uniformed four feet wide. As we climbed the ornate curving staircase to the second floor, I ran my hand along the polished banister that I could see my reflection in. Chatting about furniture placement and what colors to paint we wondered about the never-ending balcony level of the house. I had begun to feel that the lower level was five thousand square feet and so was the second.

In the family room Vi led me to a door that I assumed was a closet. Opening it she revealed a rod iron spiral staircase. Thankfully I was in flats and not my heels I followed her Pilates perfect figure up the winding steps. At the top we discovered a room that was at least twenty by twenty. Windows covered three walls. The fourth wall had a closet and full bath suite. Excitedly we headed to the window that overlooked the fenced in back yard. The French door opened with ease to the private balcony that was attached. We had a perfect view of the house behind us plus I could see some of the surrounding houses.

"Oh dear." Misgiving colored my slowly spoken words. Having followed Vi here instead of looking at a map, I hadn't really thought about the location.

"What? This house is perfect! Don't you dare ruin it!" Vi had her hands on her hips.

"There is nothing wrong with this house." I confirmed. Bracing myself I felt compelled to add. "The neighborhood across the street is a different story. No way in hell I'd live anywhere near it."

Vi frantically looked over at the stately looking brick houses. They were all lovely, manicured lawns, perfect fences. Nothing that the average person would object to or be smothered in dread from seeing a for sale sign in front of. I pointed at the red brick two story a street over. Vi looked but didn't shudder like I did at the sight of the dark brown front door. Probably because she hadn't been thrown out of it.

"That's the Swallow house." Vi's mouth dropped open. I had recanted the story to her when it happened. Her face mirrored the horror I was sure was on my own.

Three years ago, Jesse's company had been called in to assess the Swallow house. They complained of the smell of rotting meat. Particularly in the room in the garage that housed the water heater and fuse box. Despite a thorough inspection by the pest company, they couldn't find any rodents in the walls to account for the scratching on the walls. They kept firing their housekeeper because of all the dead flies. The family of four were constantly sick despite the doctors being unable to find anything wrong with them. After the third time someone beat on their door at two am, they put up security cameras. At first, they were just outside. I still shivered from the videos Jesse showed me.

The first video he showed me was the camera mounted over the garage. During the night everything was as silent as these neighborhoods get. Then suddenly the motion light came on. As soon as it flooded the empty space, there was a growling noise. The shadows seemed to ooze away from the light. Then the second feed came on. This was the front door camera. At first nothing was there, but it had been action activated. Slowly a humanoid shape formed in front of the door. It was solid black, no details just one big shadow of someone the size of the Rock wearing a cloak. Again, the growling noise. I leaned in to see if I could make out any details. BOOM BOOM BOOM. My loving husband laughed way too hard when I jumped out of my skin. The entity hit the door so hard you could see it flex with each strike of the not totally corporeal fist.

The next two cameras showed it rattling the windows of the backyard. Then the view from the back door showed the same thing that had happened at the front. BOOM BOOM BOOM. Then it was eerily quiet until the camera was triggered at daybreak by a bird flying by the garage.

Bizarrely to me, the Swallow family couldn't see the shadow figure. Only hear the growl faintly and see the door flinch from the beating it was taking. Jesse confirmed that he couldn't see it either. Unfortunately, auras weren't captured on video. One of the few times I got to give my husband a smug look and describe what was actually happening.

Not understanding what they were dealing with, they added more cameras. Both inside and out. The outside continued to show the shadow knocking at two in the morning multiple times. The inside ones footage were spine chilling. After it finished knocking, it would walk through the house. At one point it was recorded in the infant daughter's room. Standing over the crib. I could tell it was looking down at the helpless child. As a mother and a medium I was terrified for her safety. Faintly a dog barking could be heard. It reached a black smoky hand down into the crib. From the angle I couldn't tell what it was doing but the child started screaming as if her life depended on it. With a sickening chuckle the shadow disappeared when the lights were flipped on. The mother could be seen trying to soothe her baby while barely awake. What she failed to notice was the dolls all lined up on the shelf turned to watch her. Their eyes moving in bizarre and creepy as hell fashion.

There were move videos of the shadow standing at the foot of the parents bed, watching them sleep. The growling was again heard. Another one showed it standing over their older child. This time I heard more of a chanting than a growling. Some videos were of empty rooms, but things were moving around. The vacuum cleaner chased the family dog that was barking frantically at it in one of them.

After watching videos that were sure to give me nightmares, Jesse brought up pictures that had been taken. He could make out some of the auras in these but inquired what I could see in them. They made me nauseous. Most were just pictures of a family living their lives. Mom and infant floating in the pool. Never mind that shadow person lurking just over her shoulder. Baby in her highchair eating mac and cheese. Creepy ass hand with long fingernails was on her throat. A video of their five-year-old boy reciting the alphabet that had snarling and a shadow person zipping in and out of frame. One video had been taken from inside the shower. The wife had decided to take a shower while home alone. She had taken her phone in with her to listen to music while doing a treatment on her hair. While she was rinsing her hair, the shower door had started to move like it was being hit. Freaked out she started to film. Judging by the view she was sliding down the corner of the shower screaming as the door was visibly flexing in response to fierce strikes against it. The video was less than a minute long but had most likely felt like a lifetime to the poor woman. I could make a faint deep raspy voice that I knew wasn't human on it.

I replayed the footage with the shadow figure. Took screenshots to compare because I really hoped I was wrong. With the home-owners' blessing, I sent them to my mother. She would be able to see them and confirm my theory. My heart dropped when she responded. Thanking her for her quick response I told Jesse the devastating news. There were at least three different shadow beings. Most likely demons based on complaints made by the family.

Due to the severity of the situation, the Swallow house was moved to the top of the priority list. Two days later we were at the house with a local priest that was willing to work with us. When we pulled up to the house we could feel the evil leaking out of it. The family was waiting for us in the formal sitting room. It was a pleasant room full of vibrant reds and browns. Formal yet still comfortable chairs were strategically placed to facilitate easy conversations. The glass coffee table had live mums in a barrel planter. Everyone but Jesse looked at me when I jumped away from it. The norms couldn't see the ghoulish face looking at us from under the glass. It was a smallish yet definitely demonic face. The red eyes with slits for pupils was a dead giveaway. The rest of it's face had the look of meat left in the sun: gray, leathery and decomposing. Even though Jesse couldn't see the face, its aura would tell him all he needed to know. Satisfied it had scared me, it gave a cruel giggle before joining with the shadows to vanish.

Us gifted folks consulted each other then told the non-gifted to clear out. This was going to get ugly, no need to put the family in harm's way. We allowed Paul to hang back to document things. Diligently we walked the three thousand square feet of the house. The priest said his commands to leave and threw holy water. We read hymns while also throwing holy water and smudging with sage. One can never have too much holy water. As expected, the utility area in the garage was a portal. Jesse and I did our thing to seal it. While chanting a smudging, growling from the walls surrounded us. Knowing we couldn't stop; we didn't break the rhythm. The air suddenly smelt of fresh rain instead of rotted meat.

We moved on. Slowly we worked our way further in. A home office had double doors that opened to the formal sitting room close to the front door. Jesse took a sharp breath as soon as we entered it. Only the widening of Jesse's eyes alerted me to danger. I didn't have time to respond before I felt a cold disgusting hand wrap around my ankle. It lifted me off my feet. I was dragged out of the doorway by what looked like The Rock sized demon. When I had fallen, I dropped my sage and holy water. Trying to keep calm I started singing the old rugged cross. It had no effect. Mercilessly I was drug through the formal living room and thrown out the front door like I was Jazz and the demon was Uncle Phil. Before I could take in my surroundings, Jesse was at my side. I assured him I was ok, just a little bruised. Pissed, I stormed back inside. At the top of my lungs, I continued to recite scripture. Paul had picked up my smudge stick and was quoting random bible passages in our absence. With the four of us reciting and commanding, we were able to close the portal in the closet.

Disturbingly we found portals in all the bedrooms. As we worked to close them, the demons were becoming more aggressive. The armoire in the parents' bedroom fell over. Barely missed landing on Paul. The priest's rosary started to wrap itself around my neck. A canvas print of the sea cracked Jesse in the head. Still, we persisted in closing the portal.

In the little boy's room, we were all assaulted with various toys. Wall anchors prevented the furniture from being used against us. I made a mental note to start anchoring all furniture and suggesting it to anyone with a ghost problem. We were winning. Until the baby's room.

They were waiting for us there. This is where they were going to make their stand. Standing beside the bed were four shadow beings. A quick glance confirmed that even the norms could see them. That was never a good sign when they showed themselves like that. As we began our chants, the lights started to flicker. Demonic growls filled the room. Eerie laughter was interwoven with it. Claw marks were appearing in the unicorn wallpaper over the crib. They started towards the top of the ten-foot wall and slid down out of sight behind the bumpers on the crib. The dolls on the bookcase all had red glowing eyes as they launched at us. Reciting Psalms 23, I used the curtain rod that had been thrown at us moments before to knock them out of the room. Too bad the softball coach from high school couldn't see me now. Bet I'd have made the team this time.

"I walk through the valley of the shadow of death I will fear no evil." I screamed at the creepy red eyed pastel colored clown. "That means you bozo."

I kept reciting and defending us from airborne attacks. Paul to his credit kept filming. Jesse made sure to smudge every inch of the room. The priest drenched the room with holy water while commanding them to leave. During the cleansing I had moved towards the door. The Rock sized one charged me. Its footsteps echoed off the walls. Not being willing to let it take me again, I swung the curtain rod at its head. The force of the contact sent shock waves reverberating down my arms. The demon howled. Guess it missed me drenching the rod in holy water. While it was momentarily incapacitated, the rest of the group doused him and banished him. The others weren't as powerful and quickly were dispatched too.

The next morning, we had a meeting with the owners to explain the infestation. We also explained the dangers of the house. It was cleansed but it could easily have another infestation. Demons were like parasites. Once they got into a place it was hard to keep them out. We did everything we could to seal it but couldn't make any guarantees. Tragically, less than six months later the family died in their sleep due to carbon-monoxide poisoning. We weren't allowed back into the house, which kept us from discovering if it had been an accident or not. Ownership of the house had passed to the husband's brother. He was aware of the demon situation and had agreed it would be best if the house wasn't lived in. Not sure why he had put it on the market now. Hoped it was because of the economy and not because something had happened to him.

We silently but hurriedly vamoosed out of the house to our cars. Stopping only to make sure the electronic keypad was locked. I had to admit I liked this new technology that lets you look at houses without an agent there trying to talk you into a house that was right. Now you made an appointment, they sent you a code, you let yourself in, and lock it on your way out.

"Maybe not Flower Mound." Vi hugged me goodbye before she sped off in the rocket ship she was never going to let me drive.

Spine tingling, I jumped in my Jeep and hightailed it out of there hoping nothing had noticed my presence.